"Without your heels you're just a mite!"

Danny's eyes were mocking as they moved down her body to her feet.

"I may be small, Mr. Ferguson," Lizbeth said acidly, "but I function perfectly."

"I'll bet you do!"

Her cheeks flamed but she forced herself not to lose her temper. "I'll interview our leading man personally. Do you have any special requirements for Jackie Elton?"

"As long as she has maximum publicity, you decide," he replied. "I wouldn't dream of interfering."

"It's just that I realize Miss Elton has been a close friend of yours from the time your position was only that of an unknown newspaper tycoon...."

With an exclamation Danny pulled her into his arms. "And what position would I have to have before *you* would be my friend?" he demanded. Then he pressed his mouth hard on hers.

Other titles by

RACHEL LINDSAY

IN HARLEQUIN PRESENTS

Other titles by

RACHEL LINDSAY

IN HARLEQUIN ROMANCES

RACHEL LINDSAY

tinsel star

Harlequin Books

TORONTO • LONDON • NEW YORK • AMSTERDAM
SYDNEY • HAMBURG • PARIS • STOCKHOLM

Harlequin Presents edition published February 1977
ISBN 0-373-10176-7

Second printing October 1979

Original hardcover edition published in 1976
by Mills & Boon Limited

Printed in Canada

CHAPTER ONE

As always when she walked down Park Lane and saw the huge skyscraper towering towards the sky, Lizbeth Dawson could not believe her good luck in having obtained a job with National Amalgamated Television. And not just any job either but the one she had always wanted; with her own office and secretary and a salary that boosted her ego when she received it each month. The thought of this alone was enough to stop her in her tracks, and she stared mesmerised at the concrete and glass building that loomed above her.

Elizabeth Margaret Dawson was totally unlike her sedate name, being a small, quicksilver girl with a breathless way of talking that made her sound far younger than her twenty-three years. She looked innocent too, with wide-apart grey eyes staring myopically around her, and giving interested young males, of which there were many, such an intensely appraising look—due to the fact that she only saw them as blurs until they came close enough for her to focus on them—that they could not be blamed for assuming she was giving them a come-hither look instead. But they soon learned otherwise—and no mistake about it—for despite her little girl air, she had a tongue that would have done justice as a razor.

A lull in the morning rush hour traffic set her darting across the road, and breathlessly she passed through the revolving doors and dived towards one of the express elevators.

Within seconds she was walking down the corridor to her office, where her secretary was already busy on the telephone. As always when she saw Mrs Allen, Lizbeth marvelled at her luck in getting such a competent woman. At first she had worried that Mrs Allen, being so much older than herself, would not take kindly to being told what to do, but within a few days she had realised that her secretary believed she was bossing her employer rather than the other way round. It was an arrangement that had worked ideally for more than six months: from the time Lizbeth had become Publicity Officer of National Amalgamated T.V.; youngest in a line of applicants but given the job because of her excellent promotion of an hour-length documentary directed and produced by her own father. Bob Dawson had wanted her to continue working for him, but Lizbeth—anxious to stand on her own feet—had used her success to forge her own niche in the world of entertainment.

'You won't stick it for long,' her father said when she told him where she was going to work. 'You'll soon get bored promoting the trash National pump out.'

'It isn't all trash,' Lizbeth had protested at the time, though now she was reluctantly coming to the conclusion that her father was right.

'What's on the agenda today, Mrs Allen?' she asked, dropping her coat on a chair and settling in the large, black leather one behind her desk. When she sat far back in it her feet did not reach the ground and its capacious width emphasised her slightness.

'Haven't you seen the papers?' her secretary answered, and placed a couple of dailies on the desk, both folded at the relevant column on the front page.

Lizbeth bent her head and read that a major block of shares in N.A.T. had been sold to the Ferguson Press, whose chairman Daniel Ferguson intended to take an active role in the running of the company. 'I've been in the communications business all my life,' he had said at a press conference, 'and I see National Amalgamated as an additional arm.'

When asked if he intended to change the philosophy of the company, which was geared totally towards light entertainment rather than the intellectual kind, he had said he would not interfere in the day-to-day programming but would be taking a serious look at the various film series which were in the offing. 'I believe we can have mass appeal *and* quality,' he added finally.

It was this statement which gave Lizbeth pause for thought. 'I wonder if that means the axe for any of the series that have already been planned?'

'It wouldn't be a bad thing if it did,' Mrs Allen sniffed. 'If I have to watch any more films about Casanova or the Royal Henrys, I'll throw up!'

'But the viewers love it.'

'They aren't given a choice.'

Lizbeth could have argued this point, but she had a press conference at eleven to introduce two new women interviewers, and she wanted to make sure everything was ready for it.

'You're not to worry about it,' Mrs Allen assured her. 'The caterers were setting up the tables when I went to have a look. I only hope there's a good turnout. It isn't all that newsworthy.'

'There's no shortage of reporters when the drinks are free,' Lizbeth rejoined, and then gave a quick frown. 'Let's hope Mr Ferguson doesn't limit the budget on entertainment expenses. If he does, half my contacts will disappear!' She swung her legs up beneath her and the chair rocked. 'Now then, give me the letters I've got to deal with and you won't be able to nag me for the rest of the week.'

For the next hour she dealt with the many queries which, unable to be answered by the other departments, were invariably shunted over to Publicity. Much of the information required was not her job to deal with, but she found it quicker to do it than to send back the offending letters to the departments concerned. But now, looking at the huge pile of correspondence in front of her, she decided she had been too easy-going and put more than half of them aside to be returned to Current Affairs, and various other Drama departments.

'I wondered when you would stop doing other people's jobs for them,' her secretary said.

'I'm too easy-going,' Lizbeth quipped.

'You're too enthusiastic,' Mrs Allen corrected. 'You love your work so much, you don't mind how much you do.'

'You speak as if you disapprove.'

'In a way I do. I mean, look at the effort you put into getting press coverage for that ridiculous quiz game.'

'It's because it was ridiculous that it required so much work,' Lizbeth sighed. 'That's what I'm beginning to find frightening about my job. Most of it is pointless.'

'What exactly are you leading up to?'

'My resignation, I think. Not yet,' Lizbeth said quickly. 'I'm still enjoying the dining and wining and my lovely large salary, but I confess there are times when promoting starlets with low cleavages and even lower intelligence makes me want to scream.'

'Perhaps Mr Ferguson will change things.'

'He won't change the things that bring in the money,' Lizbeth said, and picking up a letter from the pile began to dictate a reply.

At eleven o'clock she attended the press conference, held in one of the small suites reserved for such a purpose on the top floor of the building. There was a far larger turn-out of reporters than she had expected, but listening to the questions put to her and her two assistants, she knew many of them had come along in the hope of learning more about Daniel Ferguson's plans for the company.

'I have no information about his plans,' she said to the sixth person who asked her. 'I just run the publicity department, and we're always the last to know!'

'I heard he's keen on building up the documentary side,' someone behind her said.

'I bet he goes all out for the American market,' someone else interposed.

'Maybe he'll do both,' the first person said: a spotty young man who represented a small but influential weekly. 'Tycoons have a habit of using profits to build up other profits.'

Lizbeth was inclined to agree with this but refrained from saying so, and with a smile moved around the room to make sure everyone had met the new women announcers.

It was one o'clock before she was finally free and, with a headache caused by cigar smoke and alcohol fumes, she decided to spend her lunch hour quietly in her office. Returning to it, she was gratified to see Mrs Allen had left her a thermos flask of coffee and a delicious-looking salad. Munching the lettuce and hardboiled egg, she immediately felt better and, coffee cup in hand, swivelled her chair round to look through the window. As always the view of Hyde Park enthralled her. Spring was already in the air though the trees were still bare. But the branches had an expectant look as if the buds were just waiting to burst open and shower the city with gold. The grass underfoot was faintly blue in the hazy light of early March and the buildings on the distant horizon were dark grey smudges against a pale grey sky. Yet those smudges held people like herself, and she wondered if they too were beset by doubts as to the value of their jobs, or did they merely see their incarceration in their tomb-like offices as a necessary part of living? There was no answer to such a question and she pushed it away and turned round to refill her cup.

She was still sipping it when Mrs Allen returned. 'I just saw Mr Ferguson,' Mrs Allen said.

'Here?' Lizbeth was surprised.

'Yes. He's lunching in the directors' dining room with the Board. I'm surprised we weren't told.'

'Perhaps he didn't want any publicity about it.'

'Do you think he's meaning to take control here?'

'He has enough shares to do so.'

'I would have thought that running his newspaper empire was enough for him,' commented Mrs Allen.

'Tycoons never have enough power,' Lizbeth said scathingly. 'Why else would he have bought into N.A.T.?'

'It's all part of the communications field,' Mrs Allen reminded her with a slight smile.

'You mean he's buying himself a monopoly,' Lizbeth snorted. 'What you read and what you see will all be controlled by Mr Daniel Ferguson.'

'Better him than a lot of others. At least he has civilised standards.'

'I never knew you were a fan of his,' said Lizbeth dryly.

'As a family the Fergusons have always represented liberalism,' Mrs Allen said defensively.

'And made a fortune out of it.'

'What's wrong with that?'

'Nothing,' Lizbeth said quickly. 'I'm just feeling a bit cheesed off in general.'

'Then don't particularise about your new boss.'

Lizbeth lowered her lids and long dark lashes, their ends gold-tipped, shading her grey eyes. 'So you do think he's going to take an active interest in the company?'

'Mr Ferguson takes an active interest in everything he controls.' Mrs Allen hesitated. 'My brother is financial editor of his Sunday paper.'

'What a dark horse you are!' Lizbeth's interest was fully aroused. 'I bet you knew about this amalgamation long before it broke?'

'I didn't,' Mrs Allen protested. 'Robert didn't know it himself.'

'But you must know something about Mr Ferguson. Does he like publicity? Do you think he'll come here every day or will he put in someone to deputise for him? I can't——'

'I know nothing about him,' Mrs Allen protested. 'Only that he's a great family man and has six children.'

'Then let's hope children's television benefits from it,' Lizbeth grinned. 'It's time some more money was spent on their programmes.'

'Most of his children are married.'

'His grandchildren, then!'

'If I know Mr Ferguson, he'll concentrate on the important programmes first; the ones that will bring in prestige as well as profits.'

Lizbeth nodded and glanced at her watch. Her afternoon was filled with appointments and if she was late for the first one it would make her late for all of them. Reaching for her coat, she draped it around her shoulders as she went down the corridor. Having a press lord with a controlling interest in N.A.T. was bound to cause changes. If they were for the better then she would remain here, but if Mr Ferguson's speech yesterday had been made to get him a favourable press report then she would definitely consider leaving. Unhappily she acknowledged that her father was right. Publicising vacuous programmes might be financially rewarding, but it was mentally enervating. Far better to do something worthwhile even if it was less well paid.

'I guess I must be a do-gooder,' she muttered, and sprinted the last few steps to catch the lift as it went down.

CHAPTER TWO

A WEEK later Tom Burdon, the Programme Controller, called Lizbeth to his office. He was a shrewd Welshman who had held his position longer than any of his predecessors.

'Take a pew, Lizbeth,' he said. 'I want to talk to you.'

'Yes, Mr Burdon,' she replied, and took a chair opposite his enormous desk.

'Mr Ferguson has just returned from the States,' he informed her. 'Two days in Hollywood, five in New York, and he's come back with co-finance for six variety spectaculars and two television series: hour-long films and twenty-six episodes each.'

'With American stars, I suppose?' Her tone relegated Daniel Ferguson's speech of a week ago to the waste-basket.

'Solely British for the two series.' Tom's beady eyes twinkled as he saw the surprise Lizbeth made no effort to hide. 'And no cops and robbers or spy stories either. So you'll have something new to get your teeth into.'

'There must be a snag somewhere.'

The Programme Controller shook his head. 'One series is semi-historical—the fictionalised lives of great politicians with an emphasis on the social reforms they put through—and the other series takes famous women through the ages: Catherine the Great, Marie Curie, Mrs Pankhurst ...'

'And these are supposed to make money?' Lizbeth asked in amazement.

'They will the way Mr Ferguson is planning them. Top screen writers are doing the plays and each episode will feature a world-famous star.'

'I fancy the political series,' said Lizbeth. 'Where does Mr Ferguson intend to put the cheesecake in that?'

'Behind every man there's a beautiful woman,' Tom Burdon grinned. 'And if there isn't, we'll write one in!'

'Back to fiction again.' Lizbeth grunted.

'Don't quibble, angel. Be thankful for small mercies.'

'At least if we're employing big stars we'll have something to publicise.'

'The producer's also doing a world-wide search for a narrator. Someone unknown whom we can build up ourselves.'

Lizbeth sniffed another new story. She could already see the headlines as queues of handsome young men formed to apply for a screen test. Perhaps they could organise some extra tests in the provincial cities? They could book a local studio and hire a local film crew. The cost would be more than covered by all the additional publicity this would generate in the provincial newspapers.

'Go and see Hugh Edwards before you start planning anything,' Tom Burdon cut across her excited thoughts. 'He's the producer. You'll find him at Elstree from Monday onwards.'

Lizbeth was relieved. She had worked with Hugh before and found him helpful.

'Is Mr Ferguson likely to make any changes

around here?' she asked, standing up.

'No heads are rolling yet, if that's what you mean, but I get the feeling he's doing first things first.'

'You mean plant new productions and cut out the dead wood later?'

The Programme Controller grinned his dismissal and Lizbeth returned to her own office and telephoned Hugh to see if she could learn any more about his search for a narrator. It turned out that he would be more than a link man between each episode and would frequently take a fictional role in them.

'I bet you'll end up with a big name,' said Lizbeth. 'This search for a new talent is so much blarney.'

'How cynical can you get!' Hugh Edwards lamented. 'We're genuinely looking for a new face—a handsome brute with sex appeal and strength.'

'Have you tested the new gorilla they have at Regent's Park Zoo?' Lizbeth questioned.

'You'll owe me an apology for that, my girl. Here am I trying to make your job easier, and all I get is disbelief!'

She laughed and hung up. The trouble was that handsome heroes usually turned out to be dead from the neck up. She pulled a face and rubbed her pencil against her cheek—the wrong end of the pencil, for it left a faint grey mark along the delicate curve of her cheekbone. Her skin was very white by comparison with the mark, for even when she was tanned in the summer she never went deeper than a pale shade of apricot. Apart from her grey eyes which were extremely beautiful and fringed by thick long lashes, the rest of her features were unremarkable: a small nose slightly tilted, a childishly shaped mouth with a full lower lip and short upper one and a small but roundly determined chin. But taken as a whole her face had a gamine charm that was heightened by her thick hair, black as night and shiny as jet, which she always wore in the same way: from a side parting to fall smoothly across her brow and down her temples to the tips of her ears, where it then softly fronded upwards. When thinking, she had a habit of pushing it away from her face with her hand, a gesture which many men longed to do for her, though the many who had tried had had their fingers slapped.

Physically she was petite; exactly five feet and perfectly proportioned, with beautifully shaped legs and the high insteps of a dancer, which she would have been had asthma not debilitated her until she was seventeen, when it had miraculously disappeared, never to return. By then she had been too old to face the exigencies of a dancer's training and, with 'A' levels behind her, had plumped for a secretarial college instead of a university. Graduating with honours, she had immediately gone to work for her father, whose own secretary had become unexpectedly ill. This temporary job turned into a permanent one and had lasted until six months ago, when she had decided she had to fly the nest in every respect. It had been a wrench to leave her father and also her parents' comfortable home in Highgate, but she knew that unless she made a clean break she would always be under her parents' domination, for they were both physically large with personalities to match. Her mother was a doctor and as well-known in her profession as her husband was in his. How either of them had come to have such a delicate-looking child had been a source of amazement for which they never ceased to be grateful. But gradually Lizbeth had found that their love was making her lazy, and regrettably but firmly she removed herself to a small flat near Camden Town.

'Watch out for the men,' her mother had warned, suddenly becoming very motherly and no longer the highly modern doctor she professed to be.

'Don't worry about men,' Lizbeth had assured her.

'I won't as long as you do!' had come the reply, and Lizbeth had hugged her mother close, all five feet eight of her, and assured her she would do exactly that.

Surprisingly there had been little to worry about, for while she had no shortage of boy-friends, none had interested her seriously.

Inexplicably she thought of this as she drove down to N.A.T. studios at Elstree a week later, where Hugh Edwards was screen-testing some two dozen males, all of whom were aspiring for stardom. Hoping to glean some good stories from them, she had decided to come down to interview them herself.

A powerful blast from a hooter nearly jerked her out of her seat, and looking in her driving mirror she saw a powerful white roadster on her tail. Lizbeth put her foot down on the accelerator and her car shot forward. Behind her the sports car did the same, hooting a demand that she move to the side and let him overtake. Though she was normally not a road-hog, the persistent hooting annoyed her into becoming one, and she resolutely refused to give way. The car behind came even closer and she pressed her foot harder on the accelerator. But she could not increase the gap between them and slowly the white car began to edge out, the hooter keeping up continuing short blasts, each one like an expletive. Annoyed with herself for not giving way in the first place, she veered to the side and waited for the car to overtake and pass her. But it did nothing of the sort. It crept alongside her and edged nearer, forcing her further and further into the kerb until her hands became clammy and the wheel seemed sticky in her hand. She glanced quickly at the car and glimpsed a man in it, clean-shaven but with thick black hair. Then she re-focused her eyes on the road, afraid that she might lose control and knowing that to do so would be dangerous, for they were barely a foot apart. The white roadster gave another loud derisive honk, then shot forward, as though having proclaimed what it thought of her, it no longer wished to bother with her.

'Arrogant idiot!' she muttered, but knew shamefacedly that she had been equally idiotic.

Arriving at the studio she soon forgot the contretemps on the road amid the welter of people she met. Hugh was in his office in the middle of a script conference, and she listened admiringly as he deftly coordinated the various ideas flung at him. He was one of the few men in the television film industry whom her father respected, and she was glad Mr Ferguson had given him the chance of working on a major production. One episode alone was costing more than her father spent making three documentaries; and then what an effort he had to get even that small sum. Fate had an unkind habit of refusing to reward the worthy, almost as though being worthy was sufficient reward in itself. It was a pity Mr Ferguson couldn't be persuaded to do something in the documentary line: real soul-searching stuff instead of the pseudo-reality he was doing now.

'Well, Lizbeth,' said Hugh Edwards, 'come to see the screen tests?'

'I thought they'd be good for a story. If you pick someone who isn't too dumb, I'd like to try and build him up as an N.A.T. personality.'

'I'm glad it's your headache, not mine.'

'It won't be a headache, if you pick an intelligent man.'

'I'm looking for beauty, not brains,' he chuckled.

'But surely he'll have to be a good actor?'

'Good actors don't necessarily need brains. Some of the best ones I know are stupid.'

She stood up. 'I'll go and look at them. Where are they waiting?'

He glanced at his watch. 'They should all be made up by now, so you'll find them in the studio watching each other's performance.'

She went down to the studio which occupied the west wing of the ground floor. The make-up rooms were to be found here too, as well as Wardrobe, which was a vast room filled with racks of clothes. At the moment it was quiet, but Lizbeth knew that once the series was underway it would be a hive of activity. It was from here that the extras' clothes came, and here that the clothes of the lead artistes were taken each night to be sponged, pressed and made good as new for the following day's shooting. She must remember to do a story about the wardrobe mistresses. They received very little recognition for their job, which often entailed long hours of overtime and much weekend work, when costumes had to be repaired.

Lizbeth entered the studio and paused. Several chippies and sparks—carpenters and electricians to those not in the trade—were moving around in front of her, but the main activity came from the far end, where lights and cameras were in position. Several groups of men were standing talking together or sitting idly on chairs. All seemed between twenty-five and thirty, and all were made up and in varying styles of dress; some in sweaters, some in open-necked sports shirts and one in a flowing burnous. They must be looking to the Middle East audience, she thought humorously, and wandered over to have a closer look at them, feeling a bit like a buyer at a slave market.

Several of the would-be stars were extremely handsome and most of them knew it, posturing and talking as though they were standing in front of a mirror. Slowly she appraised them, pausing as she came to a tall, slim man with dazzlingly fair hair and dark brown eyes. Unlike everyone around him he was sitting quietly, an expression of calm on his face. She stopped in front of him.

'Are you testing for the role of narrator?'

'Yes.' His voice was firm and his look nervous.

'Have you done any acting before, Mr——?'

'Don Colefax,' he said. 'And I've acted in repertory.'

'That's a good training.'

'For more repertory! It hasn't helped me get a part in a film yet.'

'It's early days,' she smiled.

'This is my tenth audition.'

'Never give up hoping.' She stopped. 'That sounds trite. Sorry.'

'It's true, though,' he said seriously. 'If you're an actor you have to hope—otherwise you'd give up the profession altogether.'

She remained talking with him for a few moments and then moved away to chat to some of the others. But Don Colefax was still the most handsome, though she wished he had a bit more sparkle. Still, he was nice. She must watch him when he took his screen test and see if any personality came over when he was acting.

'Is everyone here?' she asked the director.

'There are a couple more yet to come.'

'Do you fancy any one of them in particular?'

'The ones you fancy generally look like sticks on screen and the ones you'd pass over prove to light up once the arcs shine on 'em.'

'I fancy the tall blond one. Professionally only,' she added as she saw the director's grin.

'I'll let you know how he does when I see the rushes.' He signalled to his assistant, who immediately bustled forward and led one of the actors out in front of the camera.

Lizbeth watched the first few takes and then decided to leave. She waited until the camera stopped turning, the red warning light above the door went out and then she inched it open and went into the corridor. Don Colefax. She might as well make a note of his name. If he did not get the part she might recommend him to one of the directors in the London studio. She was often asked if she knew anyone to do a small part in a live production. Scribbling in her notebook as she walked, she was unaware of a man coming towards her until she bumped into him.

'I'm sorry,' she apologised, and looked a long way up into grey eyes so pale that they seemed the colour of a frozen sea in winter. Their lightness was accentuated by their being set beneath curving black eyebrows and framed by inordinately thick black lashes. The man's hair was black too and sprang back luxuriantly from a high forehead. As he half turned she saw that the hair reached the collar of his shirt, a blue shirt that matched the blue suede jacket he wore and the darker blue suede trousers. All in all a very fetching-looking man, she thought, and wished she were wearing high heels instead of flat ones.

She gave him a slight smile, but he did not return it. His mouth was firm and his nose and chin more so, the chin being somewhat square and pugnacious and the nose long and narrow, giving him a look of hauteur.

'Do you make a habit of hogging corridors as well as roads?' he inquired, and his voice, though quiet, was definitely acid. For an instant she stared at him, then realisation dawned.

'So you were the lunatic in the white car!' she gasped.

'That question, coming from a lunatic in a red one,' he said ominously, 'is not my idea of a joke.'

'I had every right to be on the outside lane,' she cried. 'I was doing fifty, and if you wanted to overtake you could have done so without blasting my head off with that childish horn!'

'That horn happens to be hand-made and exceptionally good.'

'It would sound better on an ice-cream van!'

Unexpectedly he grinned and his whole face lit up. Her temper ebbed as she saw he was far more handsome than any of the young men she had left behind in the studio. She glanced round, and only became aware of it when he said:

'Are they still doing the screen tests?'

'Yes.' She looked at his open-necked shirt and glimpsed the black hair curling on his chest. 'You'll miss your turn if you don't hurry. I suppose that's why you were driving so disgustingly.'

'I was not driving disgustingly.' He was annoyed again. 'By rights I should have reported you.'

'Count yourself lucky I didn't report you,' she retorted, her anger returning to meet his. 'For heaven's sake, save the drama for your test. It would be just my luck if you got the part.'

His eyebrows rose. 'Do you think I stand a chance?'

She glared at him. 'You've got the looks for it, and you're certainly stupid enough to be a film star.'

'Thanks!'

'Don't mention it.' She went to move past him, but he blocked her way.

'With a tongue like yours, you don't need a horn,' he said softly.

With a toss of her head she slipped past him and hurried down the corridor. She was still smarting from their exchange when she met Hugh for lunch. There were several other people at their table, all of them working on various series, and the talk was mainly shop, with some references made to Daniel Ferguson.

'He's always wanted a foot in television,' Hugh said, 'and he bided his time until he could buy into a powerful station.'

'It certainly cost him a packet,' his assistant said.

'With the new deal he's worked out with the Americans, he'll get half of that back within a year of this series going on the air.'

'Why couldn't our Board have done the same sort of deal?'

'Because they're not showmen.'

'Neither is Daniel Ferguson,' another man said. 'He's a newspaper proprietor.'

'But he understands people,' Hugh insisted, 'and that's what being a showman is.'

'Can I quote you on that?' Lizbeth asked him.

'Don't ever quote me on anything I say about our new boss! At least not until I've reached retiring age.'

Everyone laughed and Lizbeth turned the conversation to another topic. 'Are the screen tests finished yet?'

'We have a couple more to do this afternoon.'

'I saw a very good-looking blond man,' she said.

'That will be Don Colefax. I was going to use him in a film I made last year, but he looked too young. I think he'll be too young for this part too. I fancy someone about thirty, with a forceful personality.'

She thought of her encounter in the corridor and hurriedly pushed away the memory of light grey eyes. His personality wasn't forceful so much as brutal!

'Hugh knows exactly the type he wants.' The whispered comment came from the man on Lizbeth's left, who had been introduced to her as the Production Manager. 'The first episode is about Robespierre and the narrator has a wonderful cameo part in it—all sword-play and satin breeches!'

'Are you sure you aren't doing *The Three Muske-*

teers?' she whispered back.

The man chuckled. 'This is an erudite series with public appeal,' he quoted solemnly, 'and something tells me that public appeal is going to win hands down on the erudition!'

Promptly at two o'clock they left the director's dining room and Hugh promised to let Lizbeth know when he had made his choice. 'But before you release anything to the press, clear it with me,' he finished.

Promising she would, Lizbeth went on her way, not sure whether to watch any further tests or go back to London. She was standing irresolute when she had a strong premonition of being watched, and glancing round saw the man she had mentally designated roadhog.

'I thought you'd gone,' she said abruptly.

He shrugged and came closer. His hands were in the pockets of his trousers and the material was pulled across his thighs, showing their leanness and the hard muscular lines.

'Don't you care to know how I did?'

'No.' Her eyes narrowed. 'What did the director say to you?'

'I thought you said you didn't want to know.'

'It's professional, not personal,' she said coldly. 'If you were lucky enough to get the part, I'd be forced to see you again.' His eyebrows rose and she added: 'I'm Publicity Officer for N.A.T.'

'I didn't know they hired children.'

For an instant she was speechless with anger, but her momentary dumbness was long enough for her to gain control of herself and when she spoke her tone was dulcet.

'It takes a child to deal with children. And that's what most actors are.'

'Then perhaps you would lead me back to the studio? I'm afraid I've lost my way. That's actually why I was looking at you.'

'There are plenty of people to guide you.'

'But you're here,' he said, and caught her arm in an iron grip.

She debated whether to pull away, but knew he was too strong for her. A picture of herself struggling to get free flashed in front of her, and the indignity of it decided her to do as he asked.

'Follow me.'

He released her arm at once and kept pace with her as she traversed one long corridor and then another.

'The studio is at the end,' she said, pointing to it.

'Maybe I won't bother after all.' Hands still in his pockets, he teetered on his heels and looked at her. 'How about driving back with me to London?'

'I have my own car, thank you.'

'Leave it and I'll get it collected.'

'By private chauffeur, no doubt,' she said sarcastically. 'Really, you actors are all alike! You live in a world of makebelieve and never know when to stop pretending.'

'What makes you think I'm pretending?'

She tossed her head angrily and the movement made her silky hair gleam blue-black. 'I have an awful feeling you might get that part. The producer wants someone dark and intense-looking.'

'You wouldn't be kidding me, would you?'

'No,' she said shortly, 'I'm not kidding. I've just had lunch with Hugh Edwards and I know he wants someone with dark hair and strong looks.' She eyed him, making her look as impassive as though she were studying a piece of meat on a counter. 'Physically you're the right type and I can see you appealing to most of the women in the audience.'

'Except you, I take it?'

'I want more than just looks in a man.'

'Naturally. Things like brains, integrity, intelligence, ethics, charm, good manners——'

'Oh, do be quiet!' She glared at him and surprised a hurt look on his face that made her feel ashamed. After all, what right did she have to denigrate this man because he was an actor? Remembering the silly things she had said to him she wished she had not let her temper get the better of her.

'Well,' he said softly, 'what have you decided?'

'About what?'

'Me. I get the feeling you're wondering how you can help me.'

'I wasn't wondering anything of the sort,' she said coldly.

'Then you won't help me?'

'What can I do?'

'Give me a few tips on what to say to the director.'

'It doesn't matter what you say to him. It's how you look on screen that counts.' She paused, then said impetuously: 'Come to the Wardrobe Room,' and sped down the corridor.

Entering it, she was relieved to see Flora Sparrow in charge, for Flora was the most competent of all wardrobe mistresses employed by the studio.

'Can you find this man a French Revolution costume?' she demanded.

'Peasant or aristocrat?' the demand came back,

and as Lizbeth said it was definitely aristocrat, drew out blue satin breeches and a white silk jacket from a vast cupboard. 'We don't normally keep costume clothes on tap, but we're just doing a re-take on *A Tale of Two Cities.*' She disappeared into another cupboard and came out holding a rose pink jacket.

'You don't want me to get into that?' the man asked.

'Suit yourself,' Lizbeth said airily. 'But if you wear it for your test you'll stand a good chance of getting the role. Or are you so well off that you don't want the work?'

'How will this outfit help me to get it?'

'The first episode is about Robespierre and the narrator will have a cameo part in it.'

'Since you don't like me, why are you helping me?'

She looked at him, but he was bending over the jacket and she could only see his profile which gave away nothing of his thoughts. 'You might be good for the series,' she said stiffly, 'and I—I was a bit rude to you this morning.'

'It took a long time to get that apology out of you.'

'Then at least have the courtesy to accept it gracefully,' she flashed.

'I would if you had been more graceful about giving it to me in the first place.'

Her cheeks flamed. 'You really are the most infuriating man I've ever met!'

'My girl-friends tell me I'm charming.'

'The whole platoon?' she asked sweetly.

'The whole legion,' he replied, with a devilish grin, and held up the satin breeches. 'If I put on this get-up, you must promise not to come and watch me.'

Since she had planned to go back to the studio with him she was disconcerted by the request. 'I had no intention of watching you,' she lied.

'It isn't that I don't want your company,' he added, taking off his suede jacket, 'but knowing your critical eye is on me will make me nervous.'

'I didn't think any female could do that.'

'You're in a different position from the females I know. You're my guide and mentor, and you'll make me self-conscious.'

She glanced at her watch. 'Do hurry or you'll miss your test.'

He looked dubiously at the pink jacket. 'I won't feel at home in that. I think the whole thing was a mistake.'

'Don't you want the part?'

'Sure I do. But there'll be others.'

'Others!' Her voice rose to a squeak. 'Every actor in Christendom would give his eye teeth to be chosen for this series, and *you* don't want to bother! Honestly, I give up.'

'How intense you get over things,' he said admiringly. 'For me, the most important thing is to enjoy life. To have the leisure to do the things you want to do, whether it's going for a walk on the beach or lying in the grass staring up at the sun and coming to terms with yourself.'

'If you believe that, why come here for a screen test? You'd be better off meditating on a mountain top in the Himalayas.'

He laughed. 'What a girl you are for putting pigeons into pigeonholes!'

'I still haven't found one for you.' She thought of the white sports car and the determined way he had overtaken her and forced her into the side of the road in order to show off his strength. 'No, you aren't a meditator,' she reiterated, moving to the door. 'Put that on and go to the make-up room.'

'Is my nose shiny?' he asked, raising strong black brows in her direction.

'You would be improved by a touch of powder,' she said with asperity, and walked out, remembering to turn and wish him good luck before going down the corridor.

'Don't you want me to let you know the result?' he called after her.

'We'll meet again if you succeed,' she called back.

'What happens if I don't?'

She did not answer but, driving home, wished she had done so. Still, if he wanted to get in touch with her he would not be put off by not knowing her name. He knew what she did and it would be easy for him to contact her. She smiled as she remembered his expression when he had seen the pink velvet jacket. He must have looked handsome in it. It was easy to visualise him as an eighteenth-century aristocrat. There was something foreign about him. Not in his voice or bearing, which was distinctly autocratic and English, but in his dark colouring. Perhaps he was a Celt: they often had intensely black hair, though they weren't usually as tall and he was well over six feet. She had felt like a midget beside him. But tall men often liked petite girls. She thought of his comment when she had accused him of having a platoon of girl-friends. A legion, he had informed her, and she wondered now if his answer was symptomatic of his type. He was certainly good-looking enough to have a plethora of feminine company.

'Snap out of it, Liz,' she ordered herself. 'You've spent the best part of a journey thinking about a man whose name you don't even know.' It reminded her to warn Mrs Allen. She slowed and then shook her head, angry at her foolishness. Ten to one she would never set eyes on him again. It had just been an amusing episode. It could have been a fatal one, she acknowledged, recollecting the way he had forced her into the kerb. She would go on thinking of him as a roadhog. But though she tried, she was not successful, and instead kept seeing mocking pale eyes and the teasing quirk that had lifted one side of his mouth.

CHAPTER THREE

LIZBETH returned to her office to sign her mail and deal with the innumerable queries that had cropped up in her absence. Normally her job was the promotion and dissemination of news about National Amalgamated Television programmes and their stars. Information relating to the business and financial side of the company came from the Press Office, but they were so inundated with work since Daniel Ferguson had announced his major acquisition of N.A.T. shares that they had asked Lizbeth's office to help.

On her desk now were carefully worded hand-outs which her assistants had prepared, giving a résumé of Mr Ferguson's speech and some information about his private life, but there was nothing new in it beyond the fact that he was married, had six children and a host of grandchildren.

'I've never read anything duller,' she muttered to Mrs Allen. 'Seems to me Mr Ferguson shouldn't be needing a publicist. With his own newspapers, he should be able to get as much publicity as he wants.' The telephone rang and she picked it up. 'Lizbeth Dawson, Press Office,' she said automatically.

'Bob Dawson, father,' came the reply. 'I hope you're free tonight?'

'Why?'

'Because I have two tickets for the premiere of "Cardsharp" and one of your mother's patients has decide to go all broody on her. A Caesarian and twins, and she insists on being there for the delivery.'

'I don't blame her,' Lizbeth said promptly. 'It's far more exciting to watch babies arrive than see a film premiere!'

'Does that mean you don't want to come with me?' Her father sounded so disappointed that she immediately put aside all thought of a relaxing bath and an evening of Brahms.

'I'd love to go with you. What time must I be ready?'

'I'll collect you at eight.'

'Come earlier and have a snack with me. If Mother's at the hospital it will save you having something on your own.'

'I'm glad we trained you so well,' he chuckled, and hung up.

At quarter to eight Lizbeth was already dressed and waiting. A pile of open sandwiches stood on the table beside a percolator of coffee. No one looking at her would have believed she had spent a long and busy day shunting between her West End office and a film studio, for in a white lawn dress with full skirts and puff sleeves, she looked like Alice in Wonderland. Her father said it too as he greeted her with a hug and lifted her off her feet. His size and strength reminded her of Roadhog and she hurriedly busied herself with the coffee.

Appreciatively her father munched his way through the sandwiches while she sipped at her coffee and wondered why she should be feeling on edge. The ringing of the telephone almost made her jump out of her skin and her father stared at her in surprise.

'You're not expecting bad news, are you, doll?'
'No,' she said quickly, picking up the receiver.
'Hello, bossy boots,' a soft voice drawled.
'Hello, Roadhog,' she retorted promptly. 'How did the test go?'
'I'll tell you about it when we meet.'
'Are we going to?'
'Did you think we wouldn't?'
'I never gave it a thought.'
'I hope you're lying?'
Because she was, she blushed and was glad he could not see it. 'Where are you?' she asked.
'Sitting on the edge of my bath in my birthday suit. Don't you wish you were here?'
'No!'
He chuckled. '*I* wish you were here.'
'If you rang me just to say that . . .'
'Don't you know that half the females in London would fall over themselves to hear me ask them that question?'
'I'm sorry you've rung someone from the wrong half,' she said acidly.
'No. You're no mistake, Lizbeth Dawson. You're a five-foot-nothing spitfire and—' He stopped. 'But I'm not going to talk to you on the telephone. It's much more fun when I can see your eyes flash at me.'
'It's a pity we don't have a video phone,' she retorted, and hearing him chuckle, immediately felt herself grow hot. 'I didn't mean that,' she said, and heard him laugh. 'Why have you called me?'
'To ask you to have lunch with me tomorrow.'
'I'm working.'
'Then we'll have a business lunch! Meet me at

the Beachcomber's Bar at the Hilton at one. That's not far from your office.'

It was also expensive and she was dubious at letting him take her there. 'I know a very good pub even nearer.'

'So do I, bossy boots, but I still prefer the Beachcomber.'

The telephone clicked and she was left listening to the dialling tone. He had hung up so abruptly that he had given her no chance to argue with him—which was obviously his way of preventing it.

'A boy-friend?' her father inquired as she put down the telephone.

'An actor I met today. He was testing for a part in a series.'

'I thought you don't like going out with actors?'

'This one's different.'

Her father's expression made her realise what she had said and she chuckled.

'Famous last words, eh, Dad?'

'I've always had the feeling that one day you will have to eat some of them!'

'My runaway tongue,' she sighed. 'I've just been called bossy boots.'

'By the man you called roadhog?'

'Yes.' She did not offer any further explanation and was glad her father did not press the point.

'Come along, honey, or we'll be late. I thought we'd leave the car here and take a taxi. It will save the problem of trying to park in the West End.'

Even in a taxi they had to stop some distance from the cinema and go on foot along Piccadilly to Leicester Square.

'Rodney has asked us to join his party at the Savoy

afterwards,' her father said, referring to the producer of the film as they pushed their way through the throng of people milling outside the brilliantly lit foyer.

'Sounds lovely.' She blinked as several flashlights went off in her eyes. Around her people were cheering and she watched a crowd of fans throng forward to greet a celebrity emerging from the back of a limousine.

'Want to stand and gawp,' her father inquired, 'or go inside and take our seats?'

'Let's gawp,' she suggested. 'It makes a change for me to enjoy some publicity that I haven't had the headache of organising!'

A middle-aged couple came towards them with a glad cry of recognition. They were Millie and Tom Barker, a husband and wife writing team who had worked on many of Bob Dawson's documentaries.

'I didn't think musicals were in your line,' Lizbeth said.

'I wrote the screen play,' Millie replied.

'And got more for it than both of us have received for every single one of your father's films put together!' her husband added.

Bob Dawson grinned. 'Does that mean I won't be able to use you any more?'

'Unfortunately I prefer your kind of work,' Millie replied. 'But a musical now and again puts jam on the bread.'

Another cheer from the crowd drowned the rest of what she was saying and Lizbeth, knowing she was not tall enough to see over the heads of the people in front of her, waited patiently for the celebrities to come within range of where she was standing.

'She really is astonishingly beautiful,' Millie grunted.

'Who is?' Lizbeth asked, wishing she were six inches taller.

'Jackie Elton, and she's exceptionally good in the part.'

'I hadn't realised she was in the film,' said Lizbeth. I've been so busy with television since I took my new job that I never know what's going on anywhere else.'

'Shame on you,' said Millie, and continued to scan the crowd. 'I don't recognise the man Jackie's with.'

'He's supposed to be lined up as husband number two,' Tom Barker said, overhearing the remark. 'His father's sponsoring the premiere tonight.'

Millie stood on tiptoe to see better. 'So that's Danny Ferguson.'

'But he's already married,' Lizbeth protested.

'You're thinking of Daniel, the father. This is the son.'

'The one and only,' Tom spoke again. 'Six siblings and he's the only male. He'll come into a fortune when his old man goes.'

Lizbeth, tiring of hearing about people she could not see, caught hold of her father's arm as he pushed forward through the throng. It pressed all around them as several stars began to move across the foyer ready to line up to meet the royal patron who was coming to grace the occasion.

'You can get a good look at Jackie Elton now,' Millie hissed, and Lizbeth peered through a gap in the crowd to see a tall, incredibly slender girl with a sculptured-looking face and a mass of mahogany red hair. 'The colour's natural,' Millie informed her in disgusted tones. 'You'd think Nature wouldn't give her every single asset!'

Lizbeth went on looking at Jackie Elton. No wonder an old sheik had married her! She must have been the prize of his harem. Fleetingly she remembered that the marriage had lasted a bare six months. Incompatibility, Jackie had said on her return from the Middle East, and had taken up residence in a penthouse in Park Lane. Curious to see the man earmarked as husband number two—a curiosity due mainly to the fact that he was the son of the man for whom she was indirectly working—she waited while Jackie Elton threaded her way through the crowds. The girl did so, then turned to the man behind her, who was still partially blocked by several people. The star moved again and the group fell back, disclosing a broad-chested figure with a thatch of thick black hair.

Lizbeth caught her breath and Millie heard her and misunderstood the sound. 'He's quite something, isn't he? See what I mean about Jackie and luck? He's supposed to be crazy about her.'

Even if it had been to save her life, Lizbeth could not have spoken. Dumbly she stared at the couple. There was no mistake about it. The man she had mistakenly assumed to be an actor, whom she had tried to help get a part in the film series, was the son of the man who was putting up the money for it. Mortification swamped her. How could he have played such a loathsome trick on her? Of all the caddish things to do...!

'Is he—is he an actor?' she managed to say.

'No more than most handsome men are,' Millie

said wryly. 'He works with his father.'

'Hm, I should have expected it.'

'Daddy's not the easiest man to work for,' Tom Barker interposed. 'Junior had to learn the hard way—messenger boy, cub reporter, the lot.'

'Not all cub reporters make it to the chairman's office, though.'

'Lizbeth hates nepotism,' her father quipped. 'That's why she stopped working for me.'

Tom and Millie laughed and Lizbeth took advantage of it to move into the comparative dimness of the stalls. She wanted to be alone with her thoughts. Daniel Ferguson. The name reverberated in her mind like a cracked bell. What a fool he had made of her. Had he intended to keep up the act when they met for lunch tomorrow? Well, she would never know the answer to that, because she had no intention of going. How dared he ask her out when he was earmarked as Jackie Elton's next husband? The knowledge of this was more mortifying than anything else, and made it impossible for her to see the rest of his behaviour with the humour with which she would normally have regarded it.

'Anything wrong?' her father asked. 'You're sitting there as tense as an overwound coil.'

'Sorry, Dad. I was—I was thinking of some publicity I have to get organised for tomorrow.'

'Forget the office. You're here to enjoy yourself.'

Unwilling to spoil her father's evening, Lizbeth did her best to do as he said, and it was past two o'clock when she finally returned to her flat. Tiredness made her sleep the moment she put her head on the pillow, but when she awoke to her alarm call her thoughts flew immediately to Danny Ferguson.

She would leave him waiting at the Beachcomber, wondering why he had been stood up. No, she wouldn't. She would make quite sure he knew exactly why she hadn't arrived. She would send him a note and tell him so. Or could she do something more subtle? Busily she tried to figure out what, discarding one idea after another until she finally found one that brought a bitter smile to her face. He had accused her of trying to put pigeons into pigeonholes, and she would show him exactly which category she thought he best fitted.

Hastily she searched in the yellow pages of the telephone directory, scribbled down an address and then took a taxi to Holborn. Here in a side turning she found the shop she was looking for: an old-fashioned place, its owner almost as lifeless as the creatures around him.

'A stuffed snake?' he said in answer to her query. 'I'm sure I have exactly the kind you have in mind.'

Lovingly he produced a five-foot-long specimen, and with a shudder she asked him to wrap it carefully while she penned a note.

'You have shown me I am no good at putting pigeons into their correct pigeonholes. But at least I can recognise a snake when I see one.'

Without bothering to sign her name she folded the note and slipped it into the package, then took it back to the office and arranged with one of the messengers to deliver it to Mr Daniel Ferguson at the Beachcomber Bar.

This done, she tried to put all thoughts of him from her mind, but as the lunch hour drew near she found it so difficult to concentrate on her work that she abruptly terminated the conference she was holding.

Unwilling to be alone with her thoughts, she went to the staff canteen for lunch and lingered for a long while over her coffee, chatting to several producers, all of them anxious to have her publicise their own particular show. From the canteen she went on to a photographic session—it was National Amalgamated's turn to have the front cover of the weekly T.V. guide and she wanted to ensure that the shots chosen were to her liking—and it was well into the afternoon when she made her way back to her office. By now Danny Ferguson would have received the package. It was a pity she had not been able to think of a way of being there to watch his reaction to it. Anger welled up in her again at the way he had fooled her and she marched through her secretary's room and into her own, stopping short as she saw the very man she was thinking of standing beside her desk.

'About time,' he said tersely. 'Where have you been?'

'Out.'

'Do you usually accept a lunch invitation and then not go?'

'Never. But with you I made an exception.'

'Then why did you accept it in the first place?'

'I didn't know who you were then.' Remembering how she had learned the truth, her anger increased. 'You've certainly got some gall to be annoyed with *me* after the way *you* have behaved.'

'That's why I asked you to have lunch with me. I wanted to tell you the truth.'

'Oh yes?'

'Oh yes,' he said flatly, and then all at once smiled, his wide mouth curving up at the edges, one well-shaped eyebrow raised teasingly. He was not casually dressed today, she noted, but wore an impeccably tailored grey suit and navy tie. He must be playing the part of the business executive, she thought scornfully, and moved across to sit behind her desk, glad to have it as a barrier between them.

'You really are angry, aren't you?' he said. 'There are bright patches of red on your cheeks. It makes you look like a little girl.'

She tossed her head and his smile widened. 'Come on, Lizbeth, surely you can see the funny side of it? You took me for an out-of-work actor and I kidded you along. What was the harm in that?'

Only the memory of Jackie Elton enabled her to maintain her anger. But it was impossible to tell him her reason, for to have done so would have been tantamount to admitting her jealousy. But that was crazy. She didn't know him well enough to be jealous of him.

'Anyway, you have a pretty good sense of humour yourself,' he continued, 'though I must say that stuffed snake was rather overstating the case!' He leaned over the desk. 'How about beginning again? I'm free for lunch tomorrow.'

'I'm afraid I'm not,' she said coolly. 'But what are you doing tonight?'

His hesitation was slight, but she noticed it. 'Unfortunately I've already made arrangements for tonight. But if——'

'Too bad,' she interrupted. 'I'm always at my best in the evening.' She glared at him. Did he think she was so stupid that she would not discover he was tipped to be Jackie Elton's next husband, or was he so conceited that he believed a girl would be happy to go out with him regardless?

'Come on,' he insisted, and leaned closer across the desk.

His eyes were paler than she had remembered and with the light from the window shining on them, looked more silver than grey. There was no denying he was handsome, nor that he knew it. The way he was grinning at her illustrated that; as did the negligent pose of his body, hands on the desk, his wide shoulders half blocking her view. Behind him she saw the figure of a man coming through the door. For a second she did not recognise him, then the bright blond hair registered and with a cry of simulated delight she jumped up and ran round the side of the desk.

'Don!' She flung herself into his arms. Astonishment showed in his face, but luckily he caught her by the shoulders to steady her headlong flight, and she remained close to him.

'Hello there,' he said. 'I wasn't sure if you would remember——'

'Of course I remember our date,' she interrupted and, still holding his arm, pulled his forward. 'Have you met Mr Ferguson? Daniel Ferguson Junior,' she added.

'Hi,' Don said easily. 'Are you any relation to the Ferguson who's taken over this company?'

'My father.'

'Oh boy,' Don sighed, 'if only I had a father like that!'

Danny Ferguson's eyes moved away from the blond man to rest on Lizbeth. 'If you can't make lunch tomorrow, I'll try and get out of my dinner date.'

'I wouldn't dream of letting you make such a sacrifice. Will eight o'clock be all right for me to pick you up?'

'No,' she said bluntly, and rested upon Don Colefax's arm. 'I'm afraid I won't ever be free to have dinner with you, Mr Ferguson. I don't think my boy-friend would like it.' She felt Don's arm stiffen, but a quick glance at his face showed that his expression had not given her away.

'I didn't realise you had a boy-friend.' Daniel Ferguson's eyes went back to the man. 'Sorry, old man. I didn't know I was poaching.' He sauntered to the door, gave a half wave of his hand and went out.

Lizbeth waited until she heard the outer office door close before releasing her hand from Don.

'Sorry I co-opted you into being my boy-friend,' she said quickly. 'But it saved me from making a lot of unnecessary explanations.'

'Don't apologise,' Don grinned. 'I'd be delighted to make it true.' He dropped into a chair. 'But why the pretence, or do you always get rid of one boy-friend by pretending to have another?'

'Mr Ferguson isn't my boy-friend.'

'He seemed to be trying hard enough.'

'He's Jackie Elton's friend, not mine,' she added.

'I thought I'd seen the name somewhere before. It stuck in my mind because of his father being in the news recently.' Don's blond eyebrows rose. 'So Junior wants to have a bird in the bush as well as one in the hand? Nice work if you can get it.'

'Not this little bird,' Lizbeth said, and gave a perfunctory smile. 'If you ever see him again, don't tell him the truth about us.'

'What's a lie today might be the truth tomorrow!' He pulled his ear and then jumped up to come and stand by the desk. 'I actually came in to tell you I didn't get that part in the series.'

'I didn't think you would,' she said gently. 'I heard afterwards that the producer wanted somebody dark and intense-looking.'

'I've got a part in the other series, though,' he added.

'The one on famous women?'

He grinned. 'I won't be dressing in drag! I'm playing one of Catherine the Great's lovers.'

'Good for you!'

'Jackie Elton's playing Catherine,' he said casually.

'You must be joking. No T.V. series could afford her.' Lizbeth frowned. 'Anyway, it's the sort of news I'd be the first to hear. Someone must be putting you on.'

'They're not. She really is taking the part. The Assistant Producer told me. But I didn't come up here to talk about Jackie Elton. I just wanted to tell you my news and to ask you if you would care to have dinner with me.' His diffidence was unexpected and likeable and in marked contrast to Danny Ferguson's bland assurance that he could have her as another string to his bow.

'I'd love to have dinner with you, Don.'

'Tonight?' he suggested.

She nodded and scribbled down her address on a piece of paper which she handed to him.

'I've thought about you a lot,' he said, taking it. 'But if I hadn't landed some kind of part I wouldn't have had the courage to come and see you.' Seeing her surprise he added: 'You have quite a reputation around the studio, you know. They call you Miss Dynamite.'

'Among other things,' she grinned. 'Some far less complimentary.'

'Beats me how a little thing like you can hold down such a job.'

'Don't judge a book by its cover.'

'You have a beautiful cover,' he said seriously. 'But I'll tell you more about that this evening.'

He went out and Lizbeth stared moodily after him. His arrival could not have been better if she had planned it. Yet it did not alter the real state of her feelings. She was far too aware of Daniel Ferguson for her own peace of mind.

CHAPTER FOUR

For the next month Lizbeth was kept busy with personal promotions of one celebrity or another. But on the last Friday in March she was called to Tom Burdon's office and told that her department was going to be doubled in size in order to deal with the extra publicity which the Board expected her to get them for their two new film series.

'I'm glad they're finally realising the value of promotion,' Lizbeth said happily.

'Not so much the Board as Mr Ferguson,' said Tom Burdon. 'Which reminds me, it isn't official yet, but he's coming in as Managing Director.'

'I thought he was going to be Chairman?'

'That's Mr Ferguson senior. I'm talking about the son.'

Lizbeth's heart thumped erratically and then steadied. Her expression remained unchanged and Tom continued speaking.

'Obviously Mr Ferguson wants to make sure his newest toy is protected, and who better to do it than his own right hand?'

Lizbeth thought of the millions of pounds involved in the television deal. 'Some toy,' she muttered. 'I only hope sonny boy doesn't break it with his hot little hands.'

'Don't underestimate Danny Ferguson,' the Programme Controller reproved. 'He may lack T.V. experience, but he's a fast learner. And he's bright enough to have the best brains around him.'

'Like us!' Lizbeth added, smiling with an effort.

'Exactly,' Tom Burdon smiled back, and picked up the telephone, a signal that the interview was over.

Lizbeth returned to her office. Ever since coming to National Amalgamated she had looked forward to the time when the company would do a worthwhile series which she could promote with genuine enthusiasm, and she was dismayed that Danny Ferguson's unseen presence could mar her pleasure in the work ahead of her. She had to stop thinking in this way: if she didn't, she would fail in what she wanted to do.

Lizbeth's determination to show her mettle was aided by the plethora of beautiful starlets whose names were sent to her from the production department. If she couldn't get a mass of publicity from this pulchritude, she'd eat her one and only hat!

'We've never had so much sex appeal in a British series,' she said to Hugh Edwards one afternoon when he dropped into her office to discuss a profile she was doing on him for a weekly T.V. magazine.

'Thank Danny Ferguson for it,' he replied. 'He's got the Board to increase the budget so that we can buy the glamour we need. Of course he's getting his own money's worth out of it,' he went on. 'He makes himself personally responsible for each girl that comes for a screen test!'

'I bet Jackie Elton loves that!'

'Our boy knows how to deal with her. I had a script session with her yesterday and because he was there she was as sweet as sugar. Normally she queries every scene to make sure she has the camera full on her.'

'I believe Don Colefax is working for you too,' Lizbeth said, trying to change the subject.

'The big blond chap? Yes, he's doing one film in the political series and a couple more in the other one.' Hugh Edwards looked at her with humour. 'Is your interest business or special?'

Lizbeth shrugged, unwilling to commit herself verbally in a lie. In the past month she had seen Don regularly and the more she liked him, the more guilty she felt at using him. Or was she using him? After all, she had not seen Danny Ferguson again since the afternoon he had come to her office, and though she had deliberately flaunted Don at him on that occasion, her continued meetings with the young actor were more a sop to her pride than because she felt it would reach Danny's ears. Thinking it over, she decided it might be better if she began to see less of Don. He was already making serious overtures to her and she did not want him to get hurt.

'I'd like to have a look at all the scripts,' she said abruptly. 'They may give me some more ideas for publicity.'

'I'll send you copies right away, plus the names of the cast appearing in each one. We have some really old-timers playing vignettes: Lydia Perrin, Betty Leavis, Kurt Voegler——'

'Voegler!' Lizbeth was impressed. Kurt Voegler had retired from acting years ago and, like Greta Garbo before him, his name had become synonymous with an avoidance of all public appearances. 'He's always said he'll never act again,' she continued. 'What made him change his mind?'

'Not what,' Hugh smiled, 'but who. Danny Ferguson actually.'

'How did he do it?' she asked. 'He must have offered him a fortune.'

'Money wouldn't bring Voegler out of retirement, but it seems his grandson was at school with Wonderboy.'

'You sound as if you don't like our new M.D.'

'Not true,' he corrected. 'I do like him. He admits he doesn't know much about the film industry and he keeps an open mind.' The producer paused. 'He's also made me one of his advisers.'

'If you can't stop the criticism, then hire it!'

'But he also listens to it,' Hugh said seriously. 'Six months from now and he'll know the ins and outs of every single department in the company.'

'That's when it will be time for me to move on. I'd never allow him to interfere with Publicity.'

'Why should he want to do that?'

'Mr Ferguson is coming to see you,' Mrs Allen hissed, putting her head round the door. 'His secretary has just called to say he's on his way.'

'See what I mean?' Lizbeth said to Hugh.

'No, but I'm willing to sit in on the conference,' he teased.

'Not this time.' She waited until he stood up and went out before hastily powdering her nose. She was glad she was wearing one of her prettiest suits. It was a dashing red that made her skin look whiter and her hair blacker, so that to the onlooker she presented a picture of glowing vitality. Raking her hair away from her face with a small hand, she groped for her shoes—which she invariably kicked off when she sat at her desk—and had just slipped into them when Danny Ferguson came into the office with Jackie Elton.

Annoyed that she should feel so irrationally disappointed, Lizbeth gave him a crisp good-morning and received an equally crisp one in return.

'I don't think you've met Miss Elton,' he continued.

Lizbeth shook her head and smiled at the film star. Seeing her in close-up it was still impossible to fault her beauty, which was marred only by the hardness of the vivid blue eyes. She was wearing a suit too, but in a misty shade of violet that caused Lizbeth to momentarily despise her own. No Kensington boutique—however dashing—could compare with a genuine Paris model.

Carefully Lizbeth looked at Danny Ferguson. 'As a matter of fact I have an appointment to see Miss Elton at her flat on Friday to discuss the publicity we would like to do for the Catherine the Great episode.'

'I know.' His tone was off-hand. 'I came up to talk about Voegler.'

'There won't be any trouble getting promotion for Mr Voegler. Our problem will be keeping the press away!'

'It's imperative that you keep them away. That's part of the deal I have made with him.'

She gaped. 'But half his worth is the publicity he generates.'

'He has no objection to our promoting him, but he refuses to give interviews to the press. You'll have to interview him yourself, write it up and then hand it out to the papers.'

'I'm not a profesional writer, Mr Ferguson.'

'I'm sure you are a woman of many parts.'

'Possibly, but newspapers don't like receiving publicity hand-outs. If Mr Voegler is working for us, they'll want to see him.'

'You'll have to use your charm to convince them otherwise.'

Lizbeth flushed, angered by his sarcasm and seeing from the glint in his eyes that he was deliberately baiting her.

'I'll do my best, Mr Ferguson.'

'I take that for granted.' He held open the door for Jackie Elton to precede him, and with a brief nod followed her out.

Instantly Lizbeth bent to some notes in front of her, willing herself not to think of the man and the girl who had just left. There had been no reason for Danny Ferguson to see her personally to discuss Kurt Voegler. A telephone call would have done equally well—made either to her or Hugh. Yet that being the case, why had he come? Was it because he wanted to flaunt Jackie Elton at her? With an irritated murmur she concentrated on her papers. She heard the door open but did not look up.

'I'll be ready for you in a moment, Mrs Allen,' she said, and stopped as the scent of after-shave lotion told her it was not her secretary. Lifting her head, she saw Danny Ferguson.

'I forgot to let you know that Voegler will be in London on Friday,' he said. 'He's flying to Dublin on a private visit and he's changing planes at London Airport. He has an hour's wait and he's willing to see you. It should give you time to get enough to write an interesting piece about him.'

'No one has interviewed him for twenty years,' she said. 'I would feel happier if you had a proper writer doing it.'

'I've already told you he won't have a reporter.' The answer was unequivocal. 'My secretary will phone through and tell you the exact time he's arriving. Make sure you don't keep him waiting. He has a fetish about punctuality.'

She considered it unnecessary to reply to such a comment and waited for him to turn and go, surprised when he walked towards her instead and paused at the side of her desk. There must be something in what scientists said about people being attracted to each other because of chemistry. Whatever particular chemistry went to make up Danny Ferguson, it was certainly potent enough to create havoc inside her.

'How's the boy-friend?' he asked.

'Who?'

'Don't tell me you have more than one?'

Instantly she remembered and shook her head. 'Don's fine.'

'Are you serious about him?'

'Are you serious about Miss Elton?' she retorted.

'I asked the question first.'

'Will you fire me if I don't reply?'

His eyes glinted. 'I asked out of personal interest. It has nothing to do with your working here.'

'Then I needn't answer it.'

'Okay then, take it that the question is a business one.'

'How can my personal life affect what I do here?'

'Easily.' The glint in his eyes was more pronounced. 'Your job is a particularly demanding one that requires a hundred per cent of your attention. And women in love are notoriously slack!'

'Aren't men?' she snorted. 'If you're implying that I'm not doing my job properly I'm quite willing to resign.' Furiously she stood up, forgetting she was not wearing her shoes. Before she could sit down again he moved sideways, his body blocking her chair.

'What a little spitfire you are,' he said softly. 'And much smaller than I remember.' His head bent lower and his eyes moved down her body and came to rest on her stockinged feet. 'Without those three-inch spikes you're a tiddler!'

'I may be small, Mr Ferguson,' she said acidly, 'but I function perfectly.'

'I'll bet you do!'

Her cheeks flamed and she forced herself not to let him goad her into losing her temper. 'I will be at the airport on Friday to meet Mr Voegler,' she said breathlessly. 'When I've written up the interview I'll send it to you for approval before releasing it to the Press.'

'Good.' He rubbed a hand across his forehead and she noticed the faint lines that marked it. They had not been there the last time she had seen him and she decided acidly that too many late nights were making him look old.

'Do you have any particular desires about Miss Elton?' she asked, and as his eyebrows rose, wished she had phrased the question differently. 'I mean, about her publicity and the way we should promote her?'

'That's your province,' he replied. 'I wouldn't dream of interfering. Just make sure she has the maximum amount of publicity. It's the first time she's ever appeared on television, other than for an interview, and it's a feather in our cap to get her.'

'Perhaps she regards National Amalgamated with special favour. After all, you are its Managing Director.'

'I was a friend of Jackie's long before I came here.'

'I wasn't suggesting Miss Elton was your friend because of your position in television,' Lizbeth said in her sweetest voice. 'I do realise she was a close friend when you were only an unknown newspaper tycoon.'

With an exclamation Danny pulled her into his arms. 'What position do I have to be in before *you* would be my friend?' he demanded. 'An out-of-work actor again? That was the only time you showed any interest in me.'

'I thought you needed me then,' she said swiftly.

'I need you now,' he replied huskily, and pressed his mouth hard upon hers. Because he was holding her closely she could not move, nor could she feel the ground beneath her feet. All she felt was the roughness of his tweed suit, the buttons of his jacket digging into her breasts and his lips suddenly soft and rubbing gently upon her own.

'I have never known anyone to get under my skin the way you've done,' he muttered, almost inaudibly. 'You're a torment to me, Lizbeth Dawson, do you know that?'

Desperately she tried not to be influenced by his words, afraid to see them as anything other than flirtatious. 'I bet you say that to all your girlfriends!'

'Only to a favoured few.'

'You mean the ones who say no?'

His grip tightened. 'How did you guess?'

'Instinct,' she whispered, 'and if saying yes means I can get rid of you, then I'll say it now. Yes, yes, yes!'

With an abrupt movement he set her feet down on the ground. 'Your tongue is so sharp you'll cut yourself one day!'

She smoothed her hair with trembling hands and avoided his eyes.

'Turning you down normally doesn't seem to work with you, Mr. Ferguson. I'm trying to make you see that as a man you don't interest me. I know I work for you, but that doesn't give you the right to——'

'Don't say any more,' he cut in. 'I don't need to use my position to find a girl-friend.' His mouth curved into an insolent smile. 'But let me know if you change your mind.'

'Don't wait for it.'

'I never said I'd wait. I merely meant I wouldn't mind a bit extra.'

She turned her back on him. 'Good afternoon, Mr Ferguson. Don't let me detain you any longer.'

She resumed her seat and stared down at her desk. The door closed, but she did not lift her head until a couple of tears plopped on to the papers in front of her, then she leaned back and closed her eyes, wondering miserably if the scene would have ended differently if she had controlled her temper or been willing to accept what he had offered. At least a flirtation with Danny Ferguson would have given her something to remember. It might even have developed into something serious. The idea was too fanciful to consider. He was an outrageous flirt and intelligent enough to know he had everything to make him attractive to a woman: looks, personality, wealth. Yet there was a weakness in him that made him constantly seek admiration from every girl he met. She could think of no other reason why he should persist in his attentions to *her*. Her attitude obviously piqued him and he wanted to have her join the legion of lovelies who had fallen for him.

'Well, he won't get me,' she muttered. 'I'll become a nun first!'

CHAPTER FIVE

In order to prove she did not give a jot for Danny Ferguson, Lizbeth vowed to give Jackie Elton the maximum amount of publicity and arranged to see her the following day.

'I'll be home learning my script for *Colette*,' the girl said, 'so come and see me any time you like.'

Promptly at three o'clock the next afternoon Lizbeth stood outside the film star's apartment in Grosvenor Square. A maid in a black dress and white apron ushered her through a small hall into a sumptuously furnished lounge, heavy with the scent of flowers. The furniture was opulent and modern, but before Lizbeth could settle in a chair, the maid came back to tell her Miss Elton would see her in the bedroom and Lizbeth followed the girl back across the hall and into a suite. A half-open door gave on to a pink marble bathroom and the door beside it led into a bedroom that could have come straight from the Arabian Nights. Here was a room designed to match the beauty of its occupant. It was like an underwater bower with misty green walls and shimmering blue curtains, silver carpet and a bed whose cover and headboard were a mixture of all three colours.

Jackie Elton lay upon pale blue satin sheets, their pillows lace-edged, wearing a chiffon nightdress and with her hair a dark red cloud around her gleaming shoulders. It was impossible not to admire such beauty and Lizbeth could understand why Danny was bowled over by it.

'Make yourself comfortable,' Jackie drawled, and waited until Lizbeth had settled on a chair close to the bed. 'Now tell me all the wonderful things you've planned for me. I understand you're frightfully clever at your job.'

Concisely Lizbeth recounted the publicity she had arranged—and what she still planned to do—in order to promote Jackie's appearance as Catherine the Great, concluding with the promise of one magazine to feature the star on their front cover.

'How did you wangle that?' Jackie asked. 'It's one magazine that has always refused to do a thing for me.'

'I promised to write a special piece for them about Kurt Voegler.' A flash of anger enlivened the blue eyes and Lizbeth regretted her truthful answer, knowing it would have been more tactful to have said the magazine editor had had a change of heart rather than admit it was Kurt Voegler's name that had done the trick.

'Beats me what people still see in that old man,' Jackie muttered.

'He was a great actor.'

'Thirty years ago. Who cares now? If he behaved normally no one would publicise him, but because he goes around in dark glasses and has a fit every time he sees a camera he's managed to build himself into a myth.'

'Four Academy Awards are no myth,' Lizbeth pointed out.

'That's all in the past. Still, as he manages to kid the Press, I might as well use him to get myself as much publicity as I can. I'd like you to work out lots of different things for me to say about him and lots of quotes from him to me. The way he prefers *my* style of acting to the hammy old days——'

'I wouldn't want to say anything that wasn't true, Miss Elton.'

'All publicists tell lies. I mean, that's what your business is built on!'

'Mine isn't.'

'Exaggerations, then, if you prefer that word.'

'I wouldn't want to exaggerate anything about Mr Voegler. We're very lucky to have him and I don't want to antagonise him in case the company wishes to use him in the future.'

'Let Danny worry about Voegler's future. Your concern is to get me the maximum publicity *now*. You'd better fix up for me to be photographed with the old guy.'

'He won't allow photographs to be taken.'

'Get Danny to ask him.'

'You're wasting your time, Miss Elton. Mr Voegler won't agree.'

'We'll see about that.' A red-tipped hand lifted up a silver-gilt telephone receiver. She dialled quickly, without pausing to think of the number, and her face softened into gentleness as she spoke. 'Danny sweetest, I have your clever little publicist with me and I've just told her I want to be photographed with Kurt Voegler ... That's what Lizbeth said, angel, but I told her you could fix it for me. She said you wouldn't, but ... Darling, how wonderful of you!' The blue eyes slid to Lizbeth and the receiver was held out. 'Danny wants to talk to you.'

Lizbeth took the telephone and listened quietly as Danny's disembodied voice said: 'I don't think I need tell you to be tactful with Miss Elton.'

'You don't.'

'Then why argue with her when she says she wants to be photographed with Kurt Voegler?'

'Because you yourself said he wouldn't——'

'Forget what I said,' he cut in. 'Just don't argue with Miss Elton. Do everything she wants, and if you can't, let me know.'

'Very well, Mr Ferguson.' Restraining the urge to bang down the receiver, she set it gently back on the cradle.

'Danny always does as I want,' Jackie said triumphantly, and lay back against the pillows, her expression languid, as though she were remembering other times with him. It made his presence in the room almost tangible, and Lizbeth looked at the vast bed and then hastily stood up.

'I think we've discussed everything now, Miss Elton. I'll get back to the office and have the itinerary typed out for you.'

'Have a cup of coffee before you go.'

'I haven't time.'

'A chocolate, then.' Jackie bent towards the bedside table. Her breasts, large and full for someone so slim, were revealed as she did so, and she straightened without embarrassment and pulled her wrap more closely around her. 'Maybe the box is on the dressing table. Have a look for me, will you?'

Lizbeth went over to the silver-gilt table with its array of gold boxes and scent bottles.

'There's no chocolate box here,' she said.

'Try the top drawer.'

Lizbeth did so and found a box of chocolate liqueurs. She took it out, and only as she carried it over to the bed did she see the pair of cuff links resting on the lid.

'I'm sorry,' she apologised, and lifted them off.

'That's O.K.,' the film star shrugged as she took them from her. 'Danny must have left them here the other night.'

Jealousy seared Lizbeth like a red-hot poker on a steer, and the box shook in her hand. With an effort she steadied it, aware of Jackie Elton watching her.

'I'm not used to missing my lunch,' she explained. 'I get shaky if I don't eat.'

'Then it's silly of you not to have some coffee. Stay and I'll order some toast.'

'I'l grab a sandwich in the office. I really must go, Miss Elton. I've masses to do.'

Almost running from the room, Lizbeth did not slow her pace till she reached the downstairs foyer. It was ridiculous to have been so surprised by the sight of the cuff links. She was not a child. The thought made her smile wryly. Children today would have probably more easily accepted the sight of Danny's cuff links in Jackie Elton's bedroom than she herself had done. Yet why should she be surprised that he was the girl's lover? Jackie was divorced and had had innumerable affairs. It would have been illogical for them not to have consummated their love. She hailed a taxi and climbed in. But love was a word she found difficult to apply to the girl, for she doubted if she were capable of experiencing such an emotion. She was more likely to see a man as a cushion of security or an answer to a purely physical need. And Danny Ferguson could ably provide both. The knowledge was bitter, and she tried to forget it and concentrate on their telephone conversation. Even if she had not seen the links, she would have been in no doubt about his interest in Jackie, for his orders regarding her publicity had been specific. Do what Jackie wanted and if there were any difficulties, he would put things right—he no doubt put things right for all the girls who attracted his roving eye.

In the office again, she typed out a memorandum relating to the star's promotion. To the world at large it was a great *coup* for the company to obtain the services of this most expensive and glamorous star, and there would be no difficulty in getting her a great deal of coverage. The only problem as far as Lizbeth could see was to get her photographed with Kurt Voegler. The idea of trying to persuade Mr Voegler to agree to it was anathema to her. As an actor he had enormous stature and on the human level he stood for freedom and liberty, speaking out with such force against oppression that he had had to flee his country years ago. To ask him to submit to a series of cheesecake photographs with Jackie Elton was something she could not do.

It was seven o'clock before she left the office. It had been a long day and she was tired, partly from work and partly from a vague depression whose cause she refused to explore. It was a pity she had made arrangements to see Don tonight. She toyed with the idea of calling him and saying she had a headache, and then decided it was better for her to go out with him. Don's admiration was exactly the balm she needed.

Unfortunately that afternoon he had received his

script for *Catherine the Great*—in which he was playing the part of a Russian officer—and he had learned the happy news that he would be going on a week's location work in Switzerland.

'It's a pity you never took up acting,' he said. 'You'd make a far better Catherine than Jackie.'

'I've always thought it more interesting to be behind the camera than in front of it,' she replied. 'And actors are always being bossed around by other people.'

'Not if you're a good actor.'

'You still have to listen to your director, and if you can't get a part you just sit at home and wait for the telephone to ring.'

'It isn't easy to get a job as a publicist either,' he pointed out.

'True,' she conceded. 'But once you have a job it's yours for as long as you're capable of keeping it. It isn't something that only lasts for a few weeks.'

'What do you want a long-term job for?' he teased. 'You should be thinking of living in a pretty little house in Chelsea with a cat on the window ledge and a baby in a carrycot.'

'And a husband too, I hope,' she laughed.

'That goes without saying.' He caught her hand across the restaurant table. 'Would I fit the part?'

'I think you're better playing an ingénue than a husband.'

'I'd make an excellent husband if you were my wife.' He played gently with her fingers. 'I'm in love with you, Liz, you must have known that already.'

'I was hoping you weren't. Anyway, you're far too young to tie yourself down. It isn't good for your image. I'm sure your fans would prefer you to be single.'

'At the moment my fans consist of my mother and sister, and they'd prefer me to be married!' He looked at her intently. 'Is there any hope for me?'

'I don't love you, Don.'

'Because you haven't let yourself try.'

'It isn't something you can decide to do. It happens whether you want it or not.'

He looked at her quizzically. 'You sound as if you're talking from experience.'

'Not-really,' she hedged. 'But I feel that when I do meet the right man, I'll know it at once.'

'Well, until you *have* met him, I won't give up hope.'

An image of Danny came so clearly into Lizbeth's mind that it was as if a cameo had been painted on her eyeballs. She gave a shiver and Don noticed it and asked if anything was wrong.

'I'm overworked and overtired,' she lied. 'I think I'll stay in bed the whole weekend.'

'I was hoping to take you down to Somerset to meet my mother.'

'Definitely not.' She smiled to lighten her refusal and he goodnaturedly accepted the rebuff, not letting it dissuade him from putting his arms around her outside the door of her flat and giving her a hearty goodnight kiss. He was tall and strong, though not as tall and strong as Danny, nor did he kiss with the same expertise, but then, unlike Danny, he had not had as much practice. Furious that she should be thinking of Danny yet again, Lizbeth determined to try and respond to Don, and she put her arms around him, hoping his need of her would ignite a responding spark in herself. His kiss deepened, but she experienced no desire for him and remained irritatingly aware of everything around her: the dim light in the hall, the crackle of hot water in the radiator pipes, the hoot of a car in the distance and Don's breath becoming quicker as he continued to hold her. It was only as his hands went to curve around her breasts that she dropped her arms from him and pushed him away.

'No, Don, don't.'

'Let me come in with you. I won't stay long. I just want to kiss you without anyone around.'

'I'm scared of you.'

He smiled. 'I don't believe you. You know I wouldn't hurt you.'

'But I might hurt *you*. You'd want to make love to me and you'd get angry when I refused.'

'I'm not angry now, am I?'

'Only because you think I'm going to let you into the flat, and I'm not,' she said, moving quickly back into her hall and closing the door so fast on him that he had no chance to follow her.

'That's a nasty trick to play.' His voice echoed reproachfully through the woodwork.

'I'm a nasty girl,' she retorted, and heard him chuckle and give a little tattoo on her door before he walked away.

Undressing for bed, she knew that if she went on seeing Don they would eventually quarrel over her refusal to let him make love to her. He saw her behaviour tonight as a normal female ploy and would be surprised when he learned she had no intention of letting him go any further. Women in their fight for liberation weren't making it easy for girls like herself, who still wanted to remain untouched until they were genuinely in love. To like a man was not sufficient reason for her to let him make love to her, and though she knew many of her friends regarded her as old-fashioned because of this, she saw no reason to change her outlook. It was not a question of prudishness—of which several men had accused her—but a realisation of her own intensity. When she gave herself to a man she would be giving her heart and her mind, and this was not something she wished to do unless there was deep love on both sides. Having been brought up by parents who were devoted to each other and who, in spite of divergent careers, had remained faithful throughout their married life, she appreciated what a real relationship could be between a man and a woman, and for this reason was still single at twenty-three—had she been inclined—she could have been married many times over. But she had always refused to settle for second best, hoping that she would meet the right man one day. What she had not anticipated was meeting him and finding him wrong for her. A flirt who played the field; who used his prominent position to further his lustfulness.

'Get out of my mind, Danny Ferguson!' She shouted the words aloud, but somehow they lacked conviction and dejectedly she slipped into bed, hoping her sleep would not contain dreams of him, yet knowing she would be disappointed if it didn't.

The morning was a busy one, with her weekly press conference held in the reception studio. Automatically Lizbeth answered the questions fired at her and tried not to look bored. A great deal of work she did these days was routine and most of the coverage they received in the newspapers could have been obtained without the expense of sandwiches and drinks. But it was important to maintain the goodwill of the Press, for there were times when she might need them to give her extra publicity.

'Is it true that Kurt Voegler is working for you?'

The question came from Ian Donald, television critic for a leading Sunday newspaper; one of the Ferguson group, she mentally noted.

'Yes, he is,' she enthused. 'We consider we're very lucky that he's agreed to come out of retirement.'

'How much is it costing National Amalgamated to get him?'

'You must ask Mr Ferguson that!' she answered with a wide smile.

'I was hoping you'd tell me.' He inched closer and whisky breath warmed her cheek. 'If you can get me to see Voegler I'd give the interview a double spread. Any T.V. company would give their ear lobes for that!'

'So would we in the normal course of events, but unfortunately Mr Voegler won't see anyone other than me.' She paused and then made up her mind to be truthful. 'I'm going to interview him myself and then pass the story out.'

'You'll have the Union of Journalists on to you,' he quipped.

'I won't be selling it to the newspapers—just giving it to everyone as part of our normal promotion.'

'Have a heart, Liz. We're one of Ferguson's papers. Surely you can give us a bit extra or let us break the story before anyone else?'

'I haven't been told to give Mr Ferguson's newspapers any special treatment,' she said, 'but if you can clear it with Mr Ferguson, I'd be delighted to do so.'

'I'll get on to it,' Ian promised, and as he turned away to help himself to another drink, Lizbeth moved on to talk to someone else.

At noon she left her assistants to cope and returned to her own office, where Mrs Allen greeted her with relief.

'I was just going to send up a messenger for you. Miss Elton's here. I've put her in your office.'

As Lizbeth moved forwards the telephone rang and Mrs Allen picked it up. Hearing the name Voegler, Lizbeth stopped.

'It's Danny Ferguson's secretary,' Mrs Allen mouthed. 'Mr Voegler's arriving tomorrow and she has the time of his flight.'

'Make a note of it for me,' Lizbeth said, and went on into her office.

Jackie Elton was perched on the arm of a chair, one long leg idly swinging. As always she was dressed with the casual elegance that came from having spent a great deal of time and money on her appearance: her silk chiffon blouse and cream wool skirt and coat were a perfect foil for her lustrous hair and magnolia skin, whose creaminess was enhanced by the gold necklaces and chains she wore around her throat.

'I'm lunching with Danny,' she said, 'and I thought I'd pop in and see if you've started work on some of the things we talked about yesterday.'

'Not yet,' Lizbeth replied, seating herself at the desk. 'But I'm beginning on it this afternoon.'

'Good. I'm expecting a lot from you.' The comment was cool, as was the gesture with which the beige crocodile bag was opened and the typed memorandum—which Lizbeth had posted to the star last night—was taken out and unfolded.

'You've set everything down beautifully, Lizbeth. The only thing you didn't mention was my photographic session with Kurt Voegler. I know from Danny that he's arriving tomorrow.'

'Mr Voegler refuses to be photographed with anyone,' Lizbeth said steadily. 'He won't even have any photographs taken of himself!'

'I'm sure he'll make an exception of me.'

'I'm afraid I couldn't ask him to do that, Miss Elton.'

'There's no need to be afraid, darling. I'm telling you to do it!'

'I can't take orders regarding Mr Voegler from anyone except Mr Ferguson.'

'Then it's as good as done.' Jackie Elton reached out for the telephone and Lizbeth jumped up from her seat and moved out of earshot, unwilling to hear Danny's voice through the receiver and wishing she needn't hear Jackie talking to him either. The conversation was brief and after a few sentences the red head turned in Lizbeth's direction. 'Danny wants to talk to you.'

Lizbeth took the telephone. 'Yes, Mr Ferguson?'

'If I can arange for Voegler to be photographed with Miss Elton, how would you feel about it?'

Lizbeth was amazed both by the question and the fact that she was expected to answer it with the actress standing beside her. Was Danny trying to precipitate a quarrel between herself and the girl, or was he merely uncaring of either of their feelings?

'Well?' he repeated. 'Tell me what you think.'

'I think it would be wrong. The picture would be seen as a gimmick and it would detract from Kurt Voegler's stature.'

'I go along with that.'

'You do?' She was staggered by the admission.

'Certainly.' His voice was crisp. 'I've been giving your position quite a bit of thought since yesterday. You're in charge of publicity and there's no point keeping a dog and barking oneself!'

'Thank you, Mr Ferguson,' she said. 'I'll now go away and bark.' With a firm movement she put down the telephone and looked at Jackie. 'Mr Ferguson has left the decision to me and I don't think it would do either you or Mr Voegler good to be photographed together until you actually appear on the set. Otherwise it will look phoney.'

Jackie's blue eyes glittered with fury. 'Get me Danny again!'

'I don't think he'll change his mind.'

With a rude epithet Jackie pushed Lizbeth away from the desk and picked up the telephone herself. Her face was ugly with temper, though it was not reflected in her voice as she spoke to Danny. But her expression when she looked at Lizbeth again boded ill for their relationship.

'He's mad to listen to you. I know what's good for my career and——'

'You'll have all the publicity you want,' Lizbeth interrupted earnestly. 'I'll personally see that——'

'Go to hell!' the star shouted, and stormed out of the room, banging the door behind her.

For a moment Lizbeth stood where she was, appalled by the anger Jackie Elton had displayed. It was bad enough having to deal with a spoilt star, but when she was also the girl-friend of the Managing Director . . .

With a sigh Lizbeth rang for her secretary, and when the woman did not come in she muttered crossly and went into the outer office. It was empty and on top of the typewriter were two messages, one saying that her secretary had a dentist's appointment and had taken an early lunch, and the other that Kurt Voegler would meet her the following morning at eleven o'clock in the lounge of Terminal Three at London Airport.

Folding the paper, Lizbeth put it into her handbag. It was unfortunate that because of this man she had quarrelled with Jackie Elton, for she knew it was not a quarrel the star would forget. 'I've made an enemy,' she thought soberly, and though she could not see any way in which the girl could harm her, she nevertheless felt a vague premonition of evil.

Annoyed with herself for being fanciful, she went up to the top floor to see if the Press reception was over. If it wasn't, she would ask Ian Donald to have lunch with her. Even a business lunch was better than having to sit with her own thoughts.

CHAPTER SIX

INTENT on being early for her appointment with Kurt Voegler, Lizbeth did not go to the office the next morning but drove straight to London Airport. It was a warm day for early March and the sky was a bright, clear blue. The motorway was crowded but she made good time and parked her car with fifteen minutes to spare.

There were not many people in Terminal Three and she looked round expectantly for her first sight of a man whose name she had known since she was a child. Several people were sitting waiting for their planes to be called, but none of them was Kurt Voegler, and she perched on a chair and waited for him to arrive. Ten minutes ticked by and then another ten. Obviously his plane was late arriving from Switzerland. She went over to the information desk to see what time it was due in.

'It came in an hour ago,' one of the girls told her, checking her computer scanner for the numbers of the flights. 'But there's another Swissair due at noon.'

'I was definitely told eleven,' Lizbeth said. 'I'm supposed to be meeting a passenger here. It's a Mr Voegler,' she added, careful not to mention his first name. 'He's a small man with white hair.'

A look of recognition enlivened the girl's face. 'I remember him! But he was here ages ago. He came up half a dozen times to see if anyone had inquired for him. He had a beautiful speaking voice.'

'That's the one,' Lizbeth said eagerly. 'Do you know where I can find him?'

'Somewhere over Ireland, I should think. He seemed very annoyed that you weren't here to meet him and he asked if we could get him on an earlier flight to Dublin.'

Lizbeth's heart thumped. 'You mean he's gone?'

The girl walked to the other side of the counter to speak to a colleague and then came back to tell her that Kurt Voegler had left Dublin two hours before his scheduled flight at one o'clock.

'I believe he telephoned someone to see what had happened to you, because he asked me where the telephones were.'

With a murmur of thanks Lizbeth rushed to the nearest booth and dialled her office. Kurt Voegler had indeed arrived at the airport at ten and at ten-thirty had called Danny Ferguson to find out what had happened to her. This had led to Danny calling her office to find out what was going on.

'Naturally I told him you were at the airport,' Mrs Allen informed her.

'Except that I was still on the motorway,' Lizbeth muttered, and took out the typewritten note from her bag. It clearly said eleven o'clock. Unbelievable though it was, Mrs Allen must have misheard the time or else, in her hurry to get to the dentist, had typed it wrongly.

'I did no such thing,' the woman protested when Lizbeth, breathless and angry, returned to her office just before lunch. 'I made a note of it in shorthand and then copied it back in my pad.' Mrs Allen rummaged in her book and pointed her finger at a line.

There were several hieroglyphics followed by the number 10.

'But you typed eleven,' Lizbeth said grimly, and thrust the offending piece of paper towards her.

Mrs Allen stared at it and went pale. 'I'm terribly sorry, Miss Dawson. I don't see how I could have made such a mistake.'

'No one's infallible,' Lizbeth sighed. 'I only wish it hadn't happened over Mr Voegler.'

'Would you like me to explain to Mr Ferguson? I'll tell him it was my fault and——'

'Forget it. He'll just have to arrange for me to see him another time.' She turned away, stopping abruptly as she saw Danny Ferguson in the doorway. Silently he went into her office and stood by the door until she followed him in. He was pale beneath his tan and his eyes were hard as stones.

'The least you could have done was to have been on time at the airport,' he bit out furiously. 'You know the phobia he has about being kept waiting.'

'It wasn't my fault,' she protested.

'I suppose you're going to say your secretary gave you the wrong time,' he said sarcastically.

'As a matter of fact she did.'

'Didn't you check with the airport to see if the plane was going to be early?'

'No.' Lizbeth could have kicked herself for not having done so, but felt she had some excuse for it. 'I assumed Mr Voegler didn't want me to meet him before eleven,' she added. 'That's why I didn't call to check the time.'

'Seems to me you should get yourself a competent secretary,' he said nastily.

'My secretary is extremely competent. She's never

made a mistake before.'

'Perhaps she didn't make one this time.'

'What does that mean?'

'Perhaps you were deliberately late. You know the trouble I've had to get Voegler. I wouldn't put it past you to have done it purposely to annoy me!'

Fury swamped Lizbeth's control. 'If you believe I'd annoy Mr Voegler just to get even with you, then I'd better resign.'

'That's right,' he stormed. 'Take the easy way out! It's exactly the sort of thing I'd expect from you.'

'I'm not taking the easy way out,' she shouted. 'But if you think I'm so disloyal to the company that I'd use my personal dislike of you to—to ... Obviously you can't want me to stay.'

For several seconds he glared at her, then he spoke, his voice no longer loud but quiet and contemptuous. 'I have no intention of letting you leave. You've done a good job since you've been here and there's too much going on in the company to have you go right now.'

'There'll always be things going on in the company,' she retorted, 'and I'll have to leave some day.'

'Naturally,' he replied. 'But before you go, I will expect you to train someone else.'

'Then I'd better start training someone now, because I'm going the moment I can!' She tilted her head defiantly. 'You can take that as official, Mr Ferguson. I'm giving you three months' notice.'

'Suits me,' he said, and walked out.

Anger at the unjustness of his accusation buoyed Lizbeth sufficiently to get through the rest of the day, but alone in her flat that evening she gave way to a storm of tears that left her exhausted. It had been bad enough to know he saw her only as a girl to flirt with, but for him to believe she would deliberately miss her appointment with Kurt Voegler showed such complete ignorance of her character that she was appalled.

'Do let me go and see him.' Mrs Allen had made a final plea before leaving the office that day. 'If I show him the note I typed——'

'He'll think I typed it myself as an excuse for having been late,' said Lizbeth.

The older woman had looked astonished. 'He surely wouldn't think you as devious as that?'

'That's exactly what he *would* think, so you're to forget the whole thing. *I* have!' Lizbeth's expression had made it clear she meant what she said, but now, with only her own thoughts as company, she could not keep them under control. She debated whether to ring Don and then decided against it. But it was impossible to sit here by herself and on an impulse she drove to Highgate to see her parents.

'What a lovely surprise,' her mother said, putting down the medical journal she was reading and making no reference to her daughter's pallor. 'Have you had supper?'

'No, but I'm not hungry.'

'A snack, then.' Her mother went at once to the kitchen and Lizbeth looked at her father and then knelt on the rug by the fire.

'Nice having you in the house again, poppet,' he commented. 'Have you decided you're too lonely living by yourself?'

'No,' she said promptly. 'I just felt like coming up to see you. I don't always need to make an appointment in advance, do I?'

He grinned and ruffled her hair. 'How are things at N.A.T.?'

'Hectic.'

'Do you see much of Mr Ferguson, or is he out of your milieu?'

'He should be out of it,' she said carefully, 'but he interferes with everything.'

Her father chuckled. 'What you mean is that he likes to know what's going on in every department. Surely you don't blame him for that?'

'Of course not,' she said quickly. 'But he's rather —rather difficult.' She held out her hands to the fire, aware of her father watching her. 'I had a quarrel with him today,' she went on. 'It should never have happened, but ...' In a carefully modulated voice she told him of her failure to meet Kurt Voegler and of Danny's belief that she had done it deliberately. 'I've given him three months' notice,' she concluded. 'I couldn't stay on knowing he thinks I'm the sort of person who could be so spiteful.'

'You and Mr Ferguson seem to have progressed beyond the employer/employee relationship,' her father commented.

She turned sharply and her hair swung against her cheek. 'Why do you say that?'

'Because he believes you want to spite him. It isn't the sort of thing I'd expect him to think in normal circumstances.'

'Everything is perfectly normal between Mr Ferguson and myself,' she said at once.

'Then he must be paranoid if he thinks his employees only make mistakes to spite him.'

'He doesn't think that at all. It's only that with me

he——' Too late she stopped. Her father was regarding her quizzically and she knew she would have to explain a bit more. 'As a matter of fact we don't get on with each other. When I first met him I thought he was an actor looking for a job and I . . . I was annoyed with him for fooling me.' Her mother came back into the room with a percolator of coffee and a plate of delicious cold cuts.

'Go on with the story,' her father said encouragingly. 'You can't stop now.'

Staring down at a slice of cold chicken, Lizbeth recounted her first meeting with Danny and only looked up when she heard her parents chuckle. 'I don't see what's funny about it,' she protested.

'I can just picture you pushing him into the wardrobe room and ordering him into satin breeches. If you will go around trying to help lame ducks you've got to expect a few quacks!'

'It was mean of him to have pretended.'

'It was just a bit of fun,' her father said. 'What's happened to your sense of humour?'

She opened her mouth to reply and then thought better of it. Not that words were necessary, for the look that passed between her father and mother spoke volumes.

'What does he look like?' her mother asked.

'Tall, dark and handsome,' her husband replied before their daughter could do so. 'And I do mean tall, dark and handsome.'

'Obviously he doesn't appeal to Liz,' Madge Dawson said. 'That accounts for the antagonism.'

Despite herself, Liz's mouth twitched. 'Stop being so darned obvious, you two. You know very well I must have liked him when I saw him. Otherwise I wouldn't have wanted to help him get a job.'

'But you don't like him any more,' said her mother.

'No, I don't.' Resolutely she swallowed a mouthful of chicken. 'Anyway, what I think of him doesn't matter. They say he's going to marry Jackie Elton.'

'Who says?' her father asked.

'It's common gossip. Mind you, I think he's crazy. She only wants him because of his position.'

'Surely not,' her mother murmured. 'If he's as good-looking as your father says, he's the sort that would appeal to most women.'

'Jackie's not most women. She's career-mad and incapable of loving anyone except herself.'

'I think it's a good thing you're leaving N.A.T.,' her father came into the conversation again. 'If you have to waste your time promoting people like Miss Elton ... Come back and work for me, Liz.'

Instantly she was on the alert. 'Don't tell me you've managed to get the money for your new documentary?'

'Not yet, but an oil company is making the appropriate noises. I should know definitely within a week. It will mean three months in India.'

'I may take you up on that offer,' Lizbeth said, and wondered if working thousands of miles away from Danny would help her to see him in perspective and to forget him.

Driving back to her flat later that night she knew that if she wanted any peace of mind she would have to put him out of it. She was in love with a man who did not exist. Indeed, everything that Danny was she disliked. If only he weren't so handsome, nor had that strange magnetic appeal that made her conscious of him whenever he was in the same room. She was still bruised by the verbal battering he had given her for having missed her meeting with Kurt Voegler, and knew it would be a long time before she would get over it.

On an impulse she wrote to Kurt Voegler before she went to bed: a short letter apologising for the mix-up and ending with the hope that he would not judge the company harshly because of her action. Not having his private address, she sent the letter via his agent in Paris, and hoped it would be forwarded on to him.

She did not anticipate a reply and was taken aback when, four days later in her office, a call came through from Zürich. It was Kurt Voegler.

'Your apology had the ring of truth,' he stated. 'And I found your concern touching. Young girls these days don't see the necessity for apologising for anything they do—particularly to an old man.'

'I felt very guilty about it,' Lizbeth said at once, 'and I was so looking forward to meeting you.'

'How old are you, Miss Dawson?'

'Twenty-three.'

'Too young to be looking forward to meeting someone of my age—unless you are interested in antiques!'

'Great talent is ageless, Mr Voegler.'

'You were about eight when I retired, Miss Dawson. You must be speaking from hearsay.'

'On the contrary, Mr Voegler. I've seen every one of your films. There was a season of them at the National Film Theatre and my father and I saw every one of them.'

'He is a fan of mine too?'

'Very much so.' On impulse she added: 'He makes documentary films.'

'Dawson?' The resonant voice was questioning. 'Would it be the Dawson who did *Power of the Mind*?'

'Yes.' She was delighted he had heard of it.

'An excellent film. Please tell your father I enjoyed it very much, and if you are his daughter then I am doubly looking forward to meeting you. I will ask Danny to arrange another meeting for us.'

Delighted by the outcome of the call, Lizbeth continued her work with new zest, and was bent over some papers when Mrs Allen rushed in as though she had been catapulted.

'Mr Ferguson wants to see you,' she said breathlessly.

Lizbeth leaned back in her chair. 'Oh, does he?'

'*Now*,' Mrs Allen insisted. 'He's outside.'

Lizbeth's eyes widened and she hurriedly smoothed her hair as her secretary went to the door and held it open.

Danny Ferguson came into the room and stopped. He looked far more friendly than the last time they had met, and his eyes were no longer cold.

'So you *are* capable of tact when it suits you, Miss Dawson.'

'I always try to be tactful, Mr Ferguson.'

'I'm speaking about your letter to Kurt Voegler.' He rubbed the side of his cheek and she noticed how well shaped his hands were. Quickly she lowered her eyes to the blotter, deciding it was safer to focus on this than on him.

'I wrote to him because I felt he deserved an apology. I didn't want him to think I'd been deliberately discourteous.'

'Well, your gesture has paid off handsomely. I thought I'd have the devil's own job in setting up another appointment with him, but he's willing to meet you any time you like.'

'When do you want me to go, Mr Ferguson?' she asked.

'He'll be in Paris at the end of the month. You can go then.' He cleared his throat and she looked up. 'We'll be doing some location work on *Catherine the Great*,' he continued. 'I would like it covered by your office.'

Since this was Jackie Elton's film, Lizbeth could appreciate why. 'I'll arrange for one of my assistants to go. It's being shot in Switzerland, isn't it?'

'Yes, but I don't want your assistant. I'd like you to cover the assignment yourself.'

'That won't be necessary. There'll be no problem getting publicity. It's all routine stuff.'

'It won't be routine if *you* do it,' he said quietly. 'That's why I want you there.'

She stared at him and saw that his eyes had gone paler. They changed colour with his mood, glinting silver when he was angry, looking softer grey when he was teasing and a deeper grey when he was aroused. But such thoughts were dangerous and she pushed them away. 'I'll go to Switzerland if that's what you wish,' she said coldly.

'I thought you'd jump at the chance.'

'I've been there before.'

'But not with the boy-friend?'

For an instant she did not know what he meant, then remembered that Don was in the *Catherine* episode. Colour seeped into her cheeks, and the man in front saw it and looked sarcastic.

'I thought you'd forgotten that. I take it you won't make any objection to coming to Switzerland now?'

'You're the boss, Mr Ferguson, and for the next few months I still have to obey your orders.'

'For the next few months?' he echoed. 'What does that mean?'

'I gave you my notice the other day.' She was furious that he had forgotten and even more furious as she saw his look of astonishment.

'Surely you didn't mean that?'

'I never say things I don't mean.'

'Then you must be a paragon, not a female! All women say things they don't mean, when they're in a temper.'

'I'm not in a temper now, and I still want to go.'

'I'm more than willing to apologise for losing *my* temper,' he said.

'Thank you,' she murmured, 'but I won't change my mind. You believed I acted out of spite and that's something I can never forget.'

'I'll apologise for that too.' His sarcasm had gone. 'You're an excellent publicist, Miss Dawson. It would be a great shame if you left us just as you were getting things under control.'

'I still want to leave,' she repeated, knowing her only salvation lay in not seeing him again. 'I'm going to India with my father.'

'I see. In that case there's no more to be said.'

He went out, but his presence lingered as if it were indelibly impressed upon the atmosphere. With a sigh Lizbeth put on her coat and walked quickly down the corridor. What was Danny doing this evening? Jealousy was not an emotion she had ever had to contend with and she did not like what it was doing to her. Even if she wanted to stay on here, she knew it would be unwise to do so. She only hoped her father's finance did eventually materialise. Three months in India—filming in the realistic and harsh conditions her father liked—would not be easy, particularly in comparison with the way she spent her days here. But at least it would give her no time to brood, and perhaps in a new country, seeing another civilisation, she would be able to re-evaluate her own life.

CHAPTER SEVEN

Don was delighted when Lizbeth told him she was going on location with him. 'That's the only thing I didn't like about the whole idea,' he confessed. 'But now you're coming with me . . .'

'I'm going because it's my job.'

'I know that. But you can't blame me for trying to kid myself.'

'I can, if I think it's going to hurt you.'

He grinned and looked so happy that she found it difficult to believe he loved her in the same way that she loved Danny. They were having dinner in Soho, a twice-weekly habit that he refused to let her break. Occasionally she felt guilty at using him and then reminded herself that she had made it more than clear that she would never fall in love with him.

'Why so serious?' he asked, interrupting her thoughts.

'I'm worried about you,' she admitted. 'You shouldn't be wasting your time with me.'

'It isn't a waste. You're so much brainier than anyone else I know!'

'Is that what you look for in a girl?'

'Of course.' He squeezed her arm and some of her unease ebbed.

'I'd still feel happier if you went out with other girls too. Otherwise I won't believe you've taken me seriously.'

'I take you very seriously,' he expostulated. 'The trouble is, you don't take me the same way.'

'Oh Don,' she sighed, 'I wish you'd stop hoping.'

'I'll stop when you tell me you're in love with someone else.'

He caught her hand in his big, warm one and she wished with all her heart that she loved him instead of Danny. 'But I don't love Danny,' she said to herself for the countless time. 'I can't love a man I don't know. It's sexual attraction. Nothing more.'

'I'm not giving you up,' Don interrupted her thoughts. 'I intend fighting for you.'

'My Knight of the Round Table,' she teased.

'Sir Donald Galahad!' he quipped back.

'Then find a little wedge to put under *this* table. It's wobbling!'

He chuckled. 'At the prices this restaurant charges, I'll get the waiter to scramble round on the floor.'

'You shouldn't bring me to such expensive places,' she scolded.

'I didn't mean you to take that remark seriously,' he protested. 'It was a joke.'

'I know. But I've been meaning to tell you about it before. I don't like you spending all your money on me.'

'You won't let me spend all of it on you. I wish you would.'

'You know what I mean.'

'Sure I do, but you have no need to worry. This is going to be a good year for me financially. It's only March and I've already got four T.V. films lined up. That's three more than I had last year!'

'Then why not try and save something?'

'I do.' His head tilted and his hair gleamed blond in the light. At this moment he looked no older than herself, though she knew him to be six years her senior. But fair men had a tendency to look young and Don would no doubt be playing ingénu roles when he was in his forties.

'Don't look now,' he said softly, 'but Danny Ferguson has just come in with a luscious-looking bird.'

'What's happened to Jackie?'

'She's gone to New York to do a commercial. So, when the cat's away, the mouse will play.'

'You mean the rat will play.' She spoke so sharply that Don gave her a look of surprise.

'You really have it in for your boss, don't you?'

'I've never been partial to playboys.'

'They don't harm anyone as long as they stick to playmates.'

She forced herself to smile. 'Is this one a redhead too?'

'A blonde. It's safe to turn around and look. He's got his back to you.'

Lizbeth debated whether to resist the urge to turn, then with a shrug she glanced round. As Don had said, Danny had his back to her, but she would have known that commanding black head anywhere. It was bent attentively towards his companion who, though too far away to be seen clearly, was extremely decorative.

'He certainly likes variety.' Lizbeth faced Don again.

'So what? He isn't married.' Don resumed eating. 'And he doesn't care a fig for any of the girls. You just have to see him with them to know that. He smiles with his eyes only, Lizbeth. Haven't you noticed?'

'No, I haven't.'

'He's tough,' Don continued. 'Much tougher than he gives the appearance of being. He likes women and he uses his position to take his pick. I don't blame him for that—but he's no push-over for a pretty face, and if any girl sees his bedroom as a through road to stardom, she'd better think again.'

'I must get you to give me a run-down on all our executives,' she chided. 'I had no idea you were such a judge of character.'

Knowing he was being teased, he grinned and talked instead about the current political situation which, like most actors, he saw in terms of how it would affect his career.

'Hey there,' he said suddenly. 'You're not listening to me.'

Aware that she wasn't, she said hastily: 'I've just remembered something I should have done before I left the office.'

'Do you want to go back there?'

She shook her head, feeling twice as guilty because of his kind offer. On a small dais in the far corner of the room three young musicians began to play and several couples moved on to the handkerchief size dance floor. Don pushed back his chair too and Lizbeth followed him; at least if they danced she would not be required to make conversation. Comfortable in his arms, she moved around the floor, but her momentary sense of tranquillity was severely jolted as Don swung her round and she came face to face with Danny. His arms were casually about the willowy blonde he was escorting, and he was looking at her with a slight smile as she laughed at something he had said. At the same instant that Lizbeth saw him, he half turned and met her eyes. One arched brow lifted mockingly as he looked from her to Don and back again.

'Let's sit down,' she murmured to Don. 'I can see the waiter hovering by our table.'

Away from the floor she was able to relax, though she was still conscious of Danny behind her. With so many restaurants in London, what bad luck that he had chosen to come here. Determinedly she concentrated on the sweet trolley and then forced herself to eat.

'I assume we'll be staying at the same hotel in Switzerland,' Don said suddenly.

'I imagine so.'

'Are you coming alone?'

'With a stills photographer.' Lizbeth thought of the note she had received from Danny a few hours earlier. 'He wants some special pictures of Jackie.'

'She's certainly got him doing her bidding,' Don grinned.

'Maybe it's because she does his.'

'That's the first catty remark I've heard you make. You don't like her, do you?'

'No.' Lizbeth realised she had given away too much of her feelings to pretend Don was wrong. But she had to make sure he did not analyse her remark further and see *why* she disliked Jackie. 'She's so uncaring of anyone's feelings and she doesn't even put on a pretence of charm unless there are men around to see it.'

'Most women don't like Jackie,' Don said. 'It's the main reason why she'll never be an international star. It could be the reason why she'd like to get married again. If she had a husband and children, other women might see her more sympathetically.'

Lizbeth found it disquieting to think of Jackie with children, as she did the thought of who the father might be.

'Let's talk something other than shop,' she suggested.

Don signalled for the coffee. 'If it wasn't for our work we'd never have met. And think how different my life would have been.'

'Happier,' she said promptly, and again felt saddened to think she might hurt him. Yet as long as they continued to meet he would continue hoping she would fall in love with him. If she was genuinely concerned about him, she must stop seeing him. But it was impossible to do this until the Swiss trip was over. Once it was, she would ease herself out of his life.

'Care to dance again?' Don asked, and she nodded, not because she wanted him to hold her, but because she didn't want Danny to think she was trying to avoid him.

Hardly had they moved on to the floor when Danny was there too, and this time he spoke to them, introducing his escort and adding that she was working in a T.V. series.

'I've asked Belinda to give you a call in the morning,' he said, looking full into Lizbeth's face. 'She has an unusual hobby and it might be good for a piece.'

'What sort of hobby?' Lizbeth looked automatically at the girl.

'Snakes,' Belinda said.

'Two-legged ones?' Don quizzed.

'Two-legged ones are my vocation,' the girl replied, 'not my hobby!'

Lizbeth laughed despite herself. The girl was at least more humorous than Jackie Elton.

'We're going on to Annabel's,' Danny remarked. 'If you and your boy-friend would care to join us . . .'

'Don has an early call,' Lizbeth said swiftly, 'but thanks all the same.'

He shrugged and putting a casual arm around Belinda, led her off the floor.

'I wouldn't have minded going,' said Don into Lizbeth's ear. 'It doesn't do any harm to socialise with one's boss.'

'Danny Ferguson isn't your boss,' she said sharply. 'And I've no intention of kow-towing to him, even if you want to!'

Pulling away from him, she marched back to her table and Don followed and called for the bill.

'I'm sorry if I annoyed you,' he said as they drove home.

'I'm the one who should apologise,' she said contritely. 'I was very rude to you.'

'I don't care how rude you are to me. I love you.'

'You'd better start forgetting me,' she warned. 'Once I leave N.A.T. you won't be seeing me.'

'Leave N.A.T.?' Don slowed the car. 'Why are you leaving?'

'I'm going back to work with my father. We'll probably be doing a documentary in India.'

'India!' Don looked astounded and then quickly recovered himself. 'Would there be a part in it for me?'

'It's a documentary, not fiction.'

'You can't be serious about going,' he muttered.

'You'll never get another job like this one.'

'I wouldn't want it. It's been fun, but it isn't something I want to go on doing. Publicising pretty girls with snakes and handsome men with biceps soon becomes tedious.'

'There's more to it than that,' he protested.

'Not so much more.'

'Do you think of me in the same way?' he asked, stopping the car completely. 'As a boor with biceps?'

'Don't be silly,' she said quickly. 'I see you quite differently.'

'I wish you really did.' His arms came around her and his mouth pressed down on hers. Annoyed that she had not foreseen this moment, she remained acquiescent, unwilling to hurt him by struggling. But she could not respond to his touch and after a moment he became aware of it and drew back.

'I'll make you love me, Lizbeth. I want you so much.'

Knowing it was futile to argue with him, she remained silent, and he set the car in motion, not speaking until he drew up outside her flat.

'I suppose you won't let me come in for a coffee?' he said.

'You suppose right.' She tempered her words with a smile. 'Goodnight, Don, I'll be seeing you.'

'That's one thing you can count on,' he retorted and, determined to have the last word, revved the engine too loudly to hear any reply she might have made.

The next morning Lizbeth received a call from Danny's secretary, confirming his request of the night before that she obtain some publicity for Belinda Jackson. He was certainly nothing if not thorough, she thought irritably, and the only pleasure she had out of his demand was the knowledge that Jackie Elton would be furious if she knew of it.

Within an hour she had set up an interview for Belinda with a teenage magazine who thought it amusing to photograph a pretty girl with a snake. This done, Lizbeth passed the matter over to one of her assistants, feeling she herself had done as much as Danny Ferguson could expect.

His own call to her later that afternoon was another surprise in a day that had begun with one and, anticipating some further demand from him, she received instead brief praise for her effort.

'Belinda just called me,' he said. 'The photographs are so good they're putting one on the front cover.'

'That should send up your stock in her estimation.'

There was a short silence and when he spoke again his voice was very soft. 'What must I do to send up my stock in *your* estimation?'

'Nothing, Mr Ferguson.'

'You're still angry with me for the Voegler incident?'

'I'd forgotten all about it,' she said truthfully, nevertheless glad that he still remembered it, since it meant he had not guessed the real reason why she disliked him. She frowned. How ridiculous to love a man and dislike him too! She thought of Jackie and the dislike hardened into something stronger.

'Prove you aren't angry with me by coming to my office for a drink,' Danny cut into her thoughts.

'Of course, Mr Ferguson. What time do you want me?'

'Any time before you leave the office. I'll be working late anyway.'

At half past six she went up to the executive floor at the top of the building. Here were the offices of the directors and financial experts who controlled the company. Below them were housed the producers, directors and writers who were the life-blood of this complex organisation. Neither could exist without the other, yet it was the executives who had the real power: whose yea or nay could mean life or death for a project. She stopped outside the double doors that led to Danny Ferguson's office, then braced her shoulders and went in. He was at his desk, signing letters, while his secretary hovered beside him. The woman, unlike her young voice, was middle-aged, and from the few words she spoke to her employer as she took the letters from him, Lizbeth had the impression that they knew each other well.

'I don't believe you've met Miss Angers,' he said, waving a hand between Lizbeth and the woman beside him.

'Only via the telephone,' Lizbeth smiled, and saw Danny turn his head in his secretary's direction.

'Well, Miss Angers, is our Publicity Officer the dragon you thought she was?'

'Don't make mischief, Mr Ferguson,' the woman said calmly, and gave Lizbeth a warm smile as she went out.

Lizbeth perched on the arm of a chair in a casual manner that in no way echoed her feelings. The man at the desk watched her, but did not speak until his secretary had closed the door.

'I thought you'd be here earlier.'

'It's only six-thirty. Most evenings I don't leave before seven.'

'I hope we pay you overtime!'

She shook her head. 'This job is mostly overtime. That's why I get a good salary.'

'You get an exceptionally high salary,' he retorted crisply. 'That's why I doubt if you can be leaving for a better paid job.'

'I've already told you I'm leaving to work with my father. He makes documentary films.'

'Is your mother in the business too?'

'She's a doctor.' She saw her answer had surprised him and wondered why. His next remark explained it.

'That accounts for the streak of seriousness in you. I suppose you're fighting a sense of guilt at not doing something worthwhile yourself.'

'You could be right,' Lizbeth said crisply.

'Dawson,' he muttered, making a note on the pad in front of him. 'I'll arrange to see some of his work.'

'That's very good of you, Mr Ferguson.' Her tone brought his head up and even at a distance she saw the silvery glint in his eyes.

'Isn't he interested in doing T.V. work?' he asked sarcastically.

'He doesn't need you to help him.' Anger brought her to her feet. What a beast the man was! Did he think he could get round her by offering to be nice to her father?

'You have a pretty low opinion of me,' Danny Ferguson said, his voice unexpectedly resigned. 'I suppose it's because of my reputation.'

'It *is* rather well known.'

'I genuinely want to see your father's work.' He

hesitated. 'Perhaps we should both take stock of ourselves and begin again.'

'Begin what again?'

'Our meeting.' He went over to a drinks cabinet. 'Let's pretend we're meeting for the first time this evening. You know I'm the managing Director of N.A.T. and I know who you are, so there'll be no pretence on either side.' He glanced over his shoulder. 'How do you feel about that?'

'I don't know. Is—is it really necessary?'

'I think so.' He opened a half bottle of champagne and deftly filled two glasses.

'To friendship,' he said, handing her one and raising his own.

'To friendship,' she echoed, and resolutely refused to think of any other word.

'Don't go on calling me Mr Ferguson,' he said abruptly. 'I always think of you as Lizbeth.'

'I won't call you Danny in front of other people.'

'How old-fashioned you are!'

'It's a sign of respect,' she explained. 'And there's little enough of that left in this profession.'

'Using a person's surname doesn't indicate respect,' he disagreed. 'Though my father echoes your sentiments.'

'Are you like him?'

He nodded and her sympathy went immediately to his mother whom she envisaged alone in some palatial mansion while her husband, an older version of his son, squired beautiful women around town.

'What thoughts are going on behind those great big eyes of yours?' Danny asked.

'I was trying to envisage an older version of you,'

she said casually.

'Is that why you were looking so condemnatory?' He sipped his champagne. 'You have an expressive face, Lizbeth.' He topped up their glasses. 'I could answer your question very easily, but I won't. One day you'll meet my father and form your own conclusions.'

'I'd like to meet him,' she said. 'Everyone here is disappointed he hasn't been in for a visit.'

'Because I'm running the company. One thing Dad and I don't do is poach on each other's preserves.'

She wondered if this applied to their girl-friends and quickly dismissed the thought.

'Anyway, Dad isn't interested in television except as a way of investing money profitably,' Danny went on. 'Whereas I see it as an important means of communication.'

'More important than the written word?'

'Equally important.'

'Will you go back to the newspaper business?'

'One day I'll have to. It will be easier to find a replacement here.'

'I'm not sure I agree.'

'I'm glad there's something you're not sure of! You give the impression of being positive about everything.' His mouth curved in a smile. 'I suppose little women are always positive?'

'Don't go on about my size,' she snapped. 'I can't help being small.'

'I'm sure you find plenty of advantages being a pocket Venus.'

'I can't think of any.'

'Infiltration,' he said promptly. 'Think how you

can disarm your opponents by looking tiny and vulnerable and then, wham bam, in you go and bowl them over!'

'I don't see myself that way,' she confessed, and had to avoid the mischievous sparkle in his eyes as he nodded vigorously. He was flirting with her, she knew, the way he flirted with all the pretty girls who came into his life. But she had no intention of being one of the legion and she quickly set down her glass, trying to make the gesture look as though she were putting an end to the meeting.

'I'm free for dinner,' Danny said. 'How about you?' He came to stand close to her and she looked fixedly at his tie. A surprisingly austere one for such a devil-may-care character.

'I was going home,' she said huskily.

'I'm glad you used the past tense.' She lifted her head and saw that the glint in his eyes was more pronounced. How could she ever have thought him an out-of-work actor? No matter how casually he dressed he would always have a commanding presence. She must have been crazy that day at the studio.

'I ought to go home and change,' she said.

'You look lovely as you are.' He moved back a pace and let his glance travel over her.

'Until this very second,' she protested, 'you had no idea what I was wearing!'

'I never notice what you wear,' he grinned. 'I'm just conscious of those eyes of yours.' He bent his head towards her and then abruptly straightened. 'Come on, pint pot, let's go and eat. I'm starving!'

CHAPTER EIGHT

SITTING opposite Danny in the cavernous depths of one of Mayfair's leading restaurants, to which he had insisted on taking her despite her protest that she wasn't suitably dressed, Lizbeth found it difficult to believe she was not dreaming. Here he was, only a few feet away and smiling at her as if she were the only girl in his world. It was wonderful to pretend she was, and for a few seconds she let herself be transported into a makebelieve world that gave her his name and his love. Most of all his love. Warmth suffused her and she was glad the dimness of the lights prevented him seeing the blush that swept into her cheeks. But when she spoke she could not have been more prosaic.

'I do wish you had let me go home and change first.'

'I might have come back with you and then decided not to go out!'

'You're nothing if not consistent,' she quipped.

For a moment he looked put out. 'One of your failings is the way you misjudge people. Haven't you ever heard the remark about giving a dog a bad name?'

'If you're trying to tell me you're not like your reputation . . .'

'I wouldn't dream of telling you anything. The minute I tried, you would get on your high horse and ride away.'

'I'm on a chair in front of you at the moment,' she said lightly, 'so you can spin me any tale you like.'

'No more tales, Lizbeth.' He glanced over his shoulder to attract the attention of a waiter and spoke to him in an undertone. The man hurried away, returning almost at once to lead them across the room to another table set in front of a banquette. She slid on to it and Danny sat beside her, so close that she could feel the pressure of his leg.

She knew he had asked for their table to be changed and hoped he was not going to spend the evening flirting with her. If he did, she was not sure she had the strength of mind to withstand him. It was unfair that one man should have so much in his favour. Deliberately she tried to think of his failings, but there seemed to be only one: his innumerable girl-friends and, above all, the one particular one in the shape of Jackie Elton. If only she knew how serious he was about the film star!

'Let's order,' he suggested, and she accepted the outsize menu card from a waiter.

'I wouldn't even know where to begin,' she said.

'Let's choose the main course first. Are you a meat or fish girl? It's ridiculous to think I don't even know that much about you. Come to think of it, I know nothing about you other than the fact that you have a hell of a temper. No, you don't,' he said as she opened her mouth to speak. 'We're concentrating on food, remember? Now shall it be meat or fish?'

'Meat,' she said.

'They do an excellent rack of lamb here, with wine and rosemary.'

'Is Rosemary another of your girl-friends?' she asked demurely.

'Be quiet or I'll beat you!' He turned to the waiter and gave the order, choosing a first course without reference to her own taste, but assuring her in an aside that if she didn't like it, she could have something else.

The first course when it came was quenelles—tiny poached fish soufflés the size of one's thumb—in a delicate wine and cream sauce. This was followed by the lamb, which was as delicious as Danny had prophesied, and rendered even more so by the hock with which it was served.

'Is this your first meal of the day?' she asked as he ate with gusto.

'How did you guess?'

'Because you seem to prefer the lamb to me!'

'I'm saving you for my sweet!' His fingers played on her arm, sending a shiver up her spine. 'You've knocked your food back, too,' he commented. 'For a slip of a thing you eat like a horse.'

'Must you be so rude?'

'I was being complimentary,' he protested. 'I can't stand females who peck at their food.'

'I do enjoy eating,' she conceded, 'and luckily I have no weight problem.'

'No other problem either, I'd wager. You strike me as leading a very uncomplicated life.'

She bit back a sigh. If only that were true! Yet until the advent of Danny in her life it *had* been an uncomplicated one. And it would be uncomplicated again, she vowed, once she had left N.A.T. and put him out of her mind. But at the moment it seemed impossible to envisage doing this, for he was so close that a slight movement of her body and she could touch him. Indeed she could feel the warmth that emanated from him and see the individual lashes that marked those piercing, devil-may-care eyes.

'I suppose I have been lucky,' she admitted, 'and the best part was having such super parents. I've always been able to talk to them about everything and they've never tried to put their own ambitions on to me. They would have been perfectly happy if I'd wanted to climb Everest or pound a typewriter in an office.'

'Instead of which you flog yourself to death for a T.V. company.'

'It's the next best thing to writing fiction!' she smiled, and then, because the mood of intimacy was still upon her, posed her first personal question at him.

'What was your childhood like?'

'Good,' he said succinctly. 'Not as idyllic as yours, perhaps, but bearing in mind what a busy man my father was, I reckon I saw a great deal of him.'

'And your mother?'

A tender look passed over his face. 'She's a do-gooder and very forgetful with it. Our house always seemed to be full of children and animals and old people. Bearing in mind I had five sisters, you can imagine we were like a world of our own.'

'What does your mother do now?' she asked.

'More of the same thing. And with ten grand-children to add to the confusion, the house is even more hectic. My father always said he became a success because it was only by staying at the office that he could get any peace!'

Remembering Danny's assertion that he was like his father, she tried and failed to get a clearer image of Mr Ferguson Senior.

'Are your parents still married?' she asked hesitantly, and saw his look of blank astonishment. 'You said you were like your father and I thought he—I wondered if . . .'

'You're judging people again, Lizbeth. You really must stop it.' He slid closer along the seat and because she was against a side wall she could not back away from him. His leg pressed hard upon hers and the pressure of his thigh was heavy. 'Which reminds me, I must return that snake to you some time, with a little present of my own.'

'What sort of present?'

'A judge's wig.'

She threw back her head and laughed, and as she straightened he pulled her to her feet and led her on to the floor. Silently he drew her close. Never had she felt so small and vulnerable nor knew such a longing to cling to a man. She was intensely aware of his body, the feel of the muscles beneath his suit, the firmness of his chest and the hardness of his stomach against hers. He did not talk as he danced nor, in fact, did he dance so much as move languidly around the floor, his body moving slightly in time to the music which he seemed to see merely as an excuse to hold her. She knew she should protest, but she could not bring herself to do it. These were moments to be cherished for the memories they would give her. His head lowered and his chin rested on the top of her head, then his head came lower still and his cheek rubbed against hers, the faint stubble rasping her skin.

'Maybe I should have let you go home and change after all,' he whispered, 'then I could have gone home and shaved.'

'I like the feel of your skin,' she said involuntarily.

'You're tempting me to do it again,' he whispered, and proceeded to do so, moving his face slowly and rhythmically along the side of hers before he abruptly drew away and led her back to the table. Quickly he paid the bill and she was chilled by his obvious desire to terminate the evening, but she gave no sign of it as she followed him out of the restaurant to his car.

'I live in Swiss Cottage,' she said, and in silence he turned northwards, driving fast through Mayfair and down Gloucester Place and into Regent's Park. 'You obviously don't know London,' she chided. 'There was no reason to come into the Park.'

'I've come the way I want,' he replied, and drew the car into the kerb. They were in the Inner Circle, which was quieter, the silence and darkness infrequently punctuated by other cars some fifty yards away. But here, beneath the budding trees, she and Danny could have been alone in the world. She knew what he was going to do even before he did it, but she was too trapped by her own desire to stop him, and when he took her into his arms and started to kiss her, resistance was only momentary and soon she was responding to him with all the ardour with which she was capable.

'Danny,' she cried silently. 'Oh, Danny!'

It came as no surprise to her that he was as expert at making love as he seemed to be at everything else he did. But because his touch was light and deft it did not frighten her. There was no intrusion in the feel of his hands as they moved across her shoulders and down her spine, lowering the zip so that his fingers could glide across her skin and his palms could cup themselves around her breasts. She shivered at their touch, shaking with a passion she could not stem. Every part of her was trembling and the movement was echoed by his own body and the shaky way in which he kept whispering her name. Her hands stole up inside his jacket and through the fine material of his shirt she felt the dampness of his skin. With a rough movement he pulled at his tie, and catching her hand pushed it inside his shirt.

'Touch me,' he said huskily. 'Hold me, Lizbeth.'

Nervously she moved her palms across his chest, then twined her fingers in the soft tangle of hair. The feel of it made her tremble even more and her other hand lifted up to touch his head and pull it down lower. Her mouth opened beneath his and he recognised the movement of her lips as her surrender and gripped her tighter still.

'Lizbeth!' he said jerkily, and with the first sign of violence, pushed her away and swung round to stare into the darkness. 'I want you,' he muttered. 'If we go on like this I—' Again he turned to look at her, and reaching over, pulled up her zip with one sharp movement. 'Do up your jacket and move away from me. If you go on looking at me like that I won't answer for my actions.'

With trembling fingers she straightened her dress and pulled her jacket around her. Every pore in her body seemed to be alive; every nerve in her was still tingling. 'I've never ... I don't usually ...'

She stopped, embarrassed at trying to put her feelings into words and not knowing how best to do it. But he appeared to know what she meant, for without looking at her, he reached out and caught hold of her hand, touching her fingers to his lips.

'I know what you mean, Lizbeth, but luckily for you I can't say the same.' His voice was less jerky and there was faint amusement in it. 'At least I have the experience to know when to stop, otherwise by tomorrow you might have been full of regrets.'

It was a statement she could neither deny or agree with, for in all honesty she did not know how she would have felt had he not stopped his lovemaking. Would she have surrendered fully or would common sense have asserted itself at the last moment? Until now, her determination to remain inviolate had come to her aid, but with Danny she was experiencing a new emotion and had no idea what her reactions would have been. Yet one thing she did know: if she had given in to him she would certainly have regretted it in the morning, not because she would have been filled with revulsion or regret, but because in allowing him to love her she would have disclosed her own love. That was the difference between their feelings tonight. He thought in terms of lovemaking; she thought in terms of love. Bitterness rose within her as an image of Jackie Elton took shape in front of her, followed by blonde Belinda who had served to while away Danny's hours last night as she was serving to while them away this evening.

'You're expert in everything you do, Danny.' She marvelled that her voice should be so light and cool and give no indication of the turmoil within her. 'But I wasn't quite so unaware as you think. I wouldn't have let you—there was no question of our—of you'—— She buried her chin into the soft fur of her jacket. 'I wouldn't have let it go further than a kiss.' His shrug, though not accompanied by words, was eloquent enough for her to know he did not believe her, and her cheeks flamed. 'I'm not as innocent as you think,' she asserted. 'I would have stopped you in time.'

'I doubt that,' he said, and to prove his point pulled her across the seat to rest upon his chest. His arms were around her like barriers of steel, making all movement impossible. His grip tightened and she gasped with pain. He let her go at once. 'See what I mean? If I'd wanted to take you, you wouldn't have been able to fight me. Next time you'd do well to remember that.'

'I don't believe you'd take a girl who resisted you when you can get so many who wouldn't!'

'Still jumping to conclusions about my love life?' he demanded, switching on the engine.

'No jumping is necessary. You make it all too obvious. If it isn't one girl, it's another.' She was being rude to him without knowing why. It was as if his abrupt withdrawal from her—leaving her emotionally high and unsatisfied—was turning her frustrated desire into temper. 'If it isn't Jackie Elton, it's Belinda or any other little actress on the make!'

'Then how come I bothered with you? After all, if you're right about me, you've got to admit that tonight's been a waste of my time.'

'Perhaps you weren't sure it would be.'

His indrawn breath was audible above the purr of the engine and with a vicious jerk he switched into gear. 'One day I'm going to wring your neck, Lizbeth Dawson!'

Ignoring the speed limit, he raced through the

park, brakes screeching as he turned out between the gates into Avenue Road. Tersely she directed him and he stopped in a side turning in front of a white-painted gate.

'Humble but mine own,' she said, feeling his eyes on the small house. 'At least, half my own.'

He jumped out of the car and came round to open the door for her. He opened the gate too and in silence followed her up to the front door and waited until she had unlocked it.

'When I have another free evening between girlfriends,' he said casually, 'I'll give you another call.'

'Do that,' she said flippantly, and with a toss of her head, shut the door on him. Only then did the tears gush from her eyes, but she was careful to make no sound until she heard his steps recede and the engine roar and then fade into the distance. It was an unexpectedly bitter end to what had begun as a sweet evening and she wondered why it had gone so sour and whether she was more to blame than Danny.

'Of course I was to blame,' she admitted. 'I know he isn't serious about me and it makes me want to hurt him. If only I'd kept my mouth shut!'

She remembered the suddenness with which he had pushed her away from him in the car and his halting but obviously genuine reason for doing so. Why hadn't she accepted it at its face value without trying to be smart and sophisticated and pretend she did not care? If she had behaved with her usual intelligence he might have begun to see her as a person in her own right and not just as another pretty girl with whom to while away a few hours. But no, her foolish tongue had spoilt everything, and they were back on the same uneasy footing as before.

In the living-room she switched on the light, surprised to see it was only eleven o'clock. They could not have been at the restaurant for more than a couple of hours. Had Danny ended the evening early because he had wanted to come home with her? But if this had been his plan he would not have started to make love to her in the car. She was glad he *had* done so, for if they had been in the flat she would not have been able to resist him. She paused in her thoughts, but could experience no sense of wrong-doing. She loved Danny and she wanted to be a part of him. So much for all her emancipated ideas! She, Lizbeth Dawson, was as easily bowled over by a man as an innocent Victorian Miss. It was incredible to think that the training of years could disappear in one man's presence. It was a good thing there was only one Danny Ferguson in the world.

Abruptly she sank on to the settee. Only one Danny—and he was not hers to have. Yet who could take his place? Would she ever meet a man for whom she could feel the same need? 'What am I doing to myself?' she cried. 'He's taken hold of my senses. I've got to stop thinking of him!'

The telephone rang and she rushed to answer it, her pulses jerking back to normality as she recognised Don's voice.

'I thought we had a date tonight,' he grumbled. 'I've been ringing you every hour since seven.'

'It wasn't a firm date. I only said if I were free I might go out with you.'

'Where were you?'

A lie formed and then dissolved. 'I had dinner with Danny Ferguson.'

'I see.' His voice became less irritable. 'I hadn't realised you were working.'

She smiled, glad he could not see her. Thank goodness he had assumed there was a business reason for her going out with Danny!

'I suppose it's too late for me to come over for a cup of coffee?' Don said.

'Much too late. I'm just going to bed.'

She was as good as her word, but once in bed she found she could not sleep. The moment she relaxed, Danny threatened to take possession of her, causing her body to re-experience her need for him. Deliberately she started to count sheep, but this was equally disturbing, for they all had thick black hair and shimmering grey eyes, while Bo-Peep turned out to be Jackie Elton.

In the morning, heavy-eyed and listless, she walked briskly in the direction of Regent's Park, refusing to hail a taxi until the cold air had blown away some of her stupor. She stopped to buy a morning paper and saw Jackie Elton's name on the front page. 'Star refuses to wear wig to play Catherine.' This story had not come from her own department and was a completely fabricated story sent out by Jackie's own publicist. Many of them did this kind of thing, and though the newspapers generally printed them, it always made the publicist suspect, so that when a genuine news item was given, it was rarely believed. Lizbeth frowned and began to read the paragraph below the headline. 'Jackie Elton tonight confirmed that when she plays Catherine the Great in National Amalgamated's forthcoming T.V.

series, she will positively not go brunette for the part.'

'I will be giving my own interpretation of Catherine,' Jackie told our reporter when she arrived at Heathrow at midnight last night, having flown from New York to Paris earlier that day, 'and I see Catherine with red hair, like my own. It suits her passionate temperament.' (Picture on page 4.)

Lizbeth turned the pages automatically, professional interest overcoming her antipathy towards the star. The picture, as she had expected, was a good one and Jackie looked astonishingly beautiful. But it was the man to whom she was clinging that gave Lizbeth the greatest shock. For it was Danny. He had his back to the camera, but she would have recognised him anywhere. Bitterness swamped her. No reason now to guess why he had so manfully withdrawn himself from her embrace. Like Cinderella waiting for the clock to strike midnight, he knew that as the clock drew near eleven he would have to speed to London Airport to meet his beloved. And she had been foolish enough to see his withdrawal from her as a sign of respect! Rolling up the paper, she dumped it into the nearest waste paper basket, wishing she could as easily dump Danny there.

A taxi cruised past and she hailed it and jumped in. She would not work out her three months' notice. After all, she need only stay until she had trained someone to succeed her. Judy Barnes, her senior assistant, was more than competent, and if Danny was not satisfied then he could find someone else. Maybe he could hire Jackie Elton's publicist. That way he would satisfy his girl-friend in all aspects!

CHAPTER NINE

Judy Barnes was delighted at the prospect of taking over from Lizbeth, though she was the first to admit her lack of experience.

'I'd be doubtful of doing it if you left immediately,' she said, 'but if you're going to stay for a couple of months...'

'Not more than four weeks,' Lizbeth said, 'and whenever I go, you'll feel as if you're diving into the deep end.'

'I can't believe you're giving up this job. I thought you loved it.'

'I do. But I want a change.'

'Lucky for me,' Judy smiled. 'But if I take over your job, who does mine?'

'The new man I engaged.'

Judy nodded. 'Give me a couple of days to fill him into the picture.'

'Sure,' said Lizbeth. 'You can start with me on Monday.'

'Not Monday. You'll be in Switzerland that week.'

Surprised, Lizbeth pulled her diary towards her and flipped the page to the following week. 'Monday—Switzerland,' she saw written in Mrs Allen's hand, and pressed the buzzer to bring in her secretary.

'I didn't know I was on location next week,' she said.

'Hugh Edwards called and told me this morning.

He apologised for it being such short notice.'

'It's no problem for me,' Lizbeth shrugged. 'I'm sorry for their production manager. Location shooting is usually planned months ahead.'

'Not if Jackie Elton is playing the star role.' Mrs Allen's voice was dry. 'Apparently there's a clause in her contract which says no television commitment can prevent her accepting a part in a cinema film, and she starts shooting one the week after next.'

'It's worth a bit of disruption in order to have her,' Judy said artlessly. 'She's an enormous draw at the box office—as well as to our handsome Danny.'

'Don't you have work to do?' Lizbeth asked pointedly, and Judy nodded and went out.

'You look as if you didn't sleep last night,' Mrs Allen commented when they were alone.

'I didn't.' Lizbeth looked through the diary to see what dates she had before she left for Switzerland.

'You'd better hire me some ski clothes.' She scribbled some figures down on a piece of paper. 'Those are my sizes. Get me what you think is necessary.'

'The most important thing to take with you is your sense of humour.'

'That's the one thing I must leave behind,' Lizbeth said. 'Miss Elton likes to be taken seriously.'

Raising her arms in mock horror, Mrs Allen retreated, and Lizbeth forced herself to concentrate on the list of calls she had to make. She was not surprised when Don telephoned her just before lunchtime. He was shooting at Elstree and because she knew he could only speak for a few moments she was more patient with him than she would normally have been.

'You're still coming with us to Switzerland, aren't

you?' he questioned. 'I was afraid that because it was short notice you wouldn't be able to get away.'

'My boss has ordered me to be there,' she reminded him.

'I knew I had a reason for loving Danny Ferguson,' he said at once. 'As long as *you* don't.'

'I wish you'd stop going on about him!' she snapped.

'Sorry,' Don said humbly. 'But he's the one man I wouldn't like to compete with.'

'You're light years ahead of him,' she lied, and knew that if happiness could make Don a better actor, he would win the Oscar that afternoon.

As Monday drew nearer Lizbeth grew more despondent. She was not looking forward to being on location with Jackie Elton, nor having to spend a week with Don, who would expect her to be with him every evening.

She spent the weekend sorting through her clothes and, as always before she went on holiday—even a working one—came to the conclusion she had nothing decent to wear.

A quick trip to Chelsea on Saturday added to an already overflowing wardrobe, and served also to increase her confidence. She could never compete with Jackie in the beauty stakes, but there were still plenty of men who found her enticing. Even Danny had wanted her. Like a frightened horse she shied away from the memory. He had only wanted her to fill in a few free hours. Perhaps Belinda had been engaged or had begun to bore him? She wondered what he would do during Jackie's absence, and for an instant regretted her own departure to Switzerland. It would have been interesting to know if he would have contacted her. It was a foolish notion to assume even for a second. No doubt he was still angry with her for all she had said to him at their last meeting.

On Monday morning she went direct to Cromwell Road and met Don and the rest of the second camera unit who were filming the Swiss scenes. She knew most of the crew and immediately felt at ease. They took it for granted she was with Don and she was sure he had deliberately encouraged this in order to make certain that no one tried to engage her spare time. Again she determined that when they came back to England she would see less of him. Perhaps even in Switzerland she would insist on their remaining with the other members of the unit. But in the bus going to the airport she sat beside him and allowed him to shepherd her into the terminal building when they reached the airport, knowing he enjoyed feeling he was protecting her. Yet despite his size and his manliness, she considered him a boy, albeit an extremely good-looking one. It was impossible not to notice the admiring glances that followed him as they went into the departure lounge. There were still twenty minutes to take-off and she browsed at the bookstall, choosing a few paperbacks, though she doubted she would ever have time to read them.

'Here come the V.I.P.s,' Don murmured, and she glanced round and saw Jackie Elton, muffled to the eyes in mink. But it was her escort who commanded her attention as he swung along with his characteristic ease, so confident of his power that he could afford to be indolent. What was Danny doing here? Surely visitors weren't allowed through the Customs? Lizbeth was aware of him looking around and knew instinctively that he was searching for her. Forcing herself to remember she was here because of her job, she handed Don the books she had bought and moved forward to greet Jackie.

'There wasn't a single photographer outside,' the girl complained as she came within earshot.

'Our own man was there,' said Lizbeth, 'and he'll see the papers are all covered. But you'll be meeting the foreign press at Zürich airport.'

'Let's hope I'm not airsick! I prefer to be interviewed before I fly, not afterwards. If you'd had any sense you would have checked with me.'

Lizbeth bit her lip. Though she did not feel she had been lacking in her duty she wished she had done as Jackie had said. Danny thought the same, for he favoured her with a hard stare.

'I expect you to give Miss Elton your maximum attention,' he drawled. 'Everyone else takes second place. And that means your boy-friend too.'

Lizbeth was so angry that she spoke without thinking. 'You do have women watching television as well as men, Mr Ferguson.'

The silence was electric, then Danny shrugged. 'Point taken. I apologise.'

'You two are always fighting and apologising to each other.' Jackie was suddenly in a good mood. 'Come and buy me some magazines, darling. I haven't anything to read.'

'Aren't I entertainment enough?' he asked.

'More than enough. But I do like to take it easy some time!'

He laughed and drew her over to the bookstall, leaving Lizbeth to accept with bitter frustration the knowledge that he was coming to Switzerland with them. Why hadn't she realised the possibility of this? Naturally it would be an ideal opportunity for him to spend time with the star, and what could be more glamorous than a gay Swiss setting in the snow-covered mountains?

Throughout the journey Lizbeth was able to keep out of Danny's way though she was conscious of his presence the whole time. Because of union rules, they were all travelling first class, and she found herself sitting directly behind him and Jackie. The noise of the engines prevented her from hearing their conversation, but she could not avoid the intimate gestures the girl lavished on him, her hand resting frequently on his arm, fluttering over his cheek or touching his leg. Don was amused by it all and Lizbeth forced herself to appear the same, though she seethed with jealousy and hated herself for it. This did nothing to encourage her peace of mind and her nerves were stretched to breaking point by the time they touched down at Zürich.

Luckily the flight had been a good one and Jackie posed happily for the photographers, giving them lots of amusing quotes about Catherine's character; stressing the woman's love life and thereby assuring that when the series was shown they would have a record audience.

'Nobody understands the value of publicity better than Jackie,' Danny said in an aside to Lizbeth.

'Perhaps you'd better get her to take my job!'

'How would you feel about taking hers?'

'I can't act.'

'I wasn't thinking of that job.' His voice was low. 'But you seem to have given her a special role in my life and I wonder how you would feel about taking it over.'

'Very funny,' she snapped, and turned her back on him. But he side-stepped in front of her and she found herself facing him again.

'Don't ever turn your back on me, Lizbeth.' His voice was quiet, but she shivered at the white hot anger in it. 'Nobody does that to me when I'm talking to them. Not even a woman.'

'I didn't realise you felt so strongly about rejection!'

'I don't.' His voice was still quiet. 'But I do feel strongly about bad manners.'

Her heart was pounding so loudly that she could hardly hear him and she was overcome by such a sense of loss that she wanted to burst into tears. Her expression must have given away something of her feelings, for he put his hand on her arm.

'What's wrong. Lizbeth? Are you feeling ill?'

'Slightly sick,' she mumbled. 'It's warm in here.'

She did indeed feel nauseous, but knew it had nothing to do with heat. Rather it stemmed from the proximity of this man who was wreaking havoc with her composure. Luckily he took her words at their face value and put his hand around her shoulders, half leading, half carrying her to a seat. With a swift movement he pushed her head down on to her lap.

'Keep like that,' he ordered. 'I won't be a minute!'

In half that time he returned with a glass of brandy. 'Drink up, Lizbeth. It will make you feel better.'

Obediently she took a sip.

'Close your eyes again,' he advised. 'I'll let you know when we're ready to leave.'

She was glad to obey him and remained quietly in her chair, only half aware of the confusion around her. The airport was packed and an English couple who sat down next to her assured her that the early spring was the best time to go skiing, for one then had sunshine as well as snow.

'I'm not going skiing,' she told them. 'I'm here to work.' Behind her she was aware of a commotion and knew Jackie had swept by, still surrounded by photographers and a small but swelling crowd of fans.

'Gosh,' said the young man beside her. 'She's even more beautiful off screen than on.'

'What about the blond man with her?' his girl-friend retorted.

Lizbeth found it strange to hear Don referred to in those terms and wished she could see him in the same way. How uncomplicated her future would be if she could! She stood up, glad to find she felt better, and went off to join the film unit.

'I thought I told you to stay where you were?' Danny was beside her and she saw that Jackie was watching them. The last thing in the world she wanted was to excite the star's jealousy. This week was going to be difficult enough without that. Instinctively she turned to Don, accepting that she would have to use him as a means of disarming the girl's suspicions. It was interesting that Jackie, for all her beauty and Danny's admiration of her, should be jealous of another woman, and she wondered if it stemmed from insecurity or possessiveness. Possibly it was a mixture of both.

From Zürich they travelled by train to Arosa, climbing ever higher until they reached a landscape totally covered by snow. The ascent was so steep that Lizbeth's heart was frequently in her mouth, but most of the passengers seemed unperturbed and people got off and on at the small wayside halts, all of them dressed in ski clothes, many of them carrying gaily coloured skis.

It was dusk by the time they reached Arosa. This was the end of the line for the train and it stood puffing gently while passengers disgorged from its bowels and slipped and skidded away to waiting cars and horse-drawn carriages. Two small buses were waiting to take them to their hotel; one took all their luggage and camera equipment and the other took the crew and herself, though Jackie and Danny went on their own in a car.

The assistant director watched them go and gave Lizbeth a slight smile. 'I'm glad Ferguson is here. He's the only man who can control her. She's impossible otherwise.'

Lizbeth was surprised. 'I always thought she was very professional on the set.'

'A film set, maybe. But when it comes to television she feels she's doing us a big favour.'

'She's being highly paid for the favour!'

'Try telling her that! If it weren't for Ferguson she would never have agreed to do it.'

'Maybe he's giving her more than money,' one of the camera crew interposed.

'I should be so lucky,' another man said, and there was ribald laughter.

Lizbeth climbed hastily into the bus and as they drove up the steep village street, their chained tyres gripping the icy road, the engine working overtime and the windows so steamy from the warmth inside and the cold outside that it was almost impossible to discern anything of the village itself. At the top the road widened into a plateau. Here stood the ski school and the large huts where one could hire equipment. Beyond it were the lights of a large hotel, but the bus swept past and then swung abruptly right between a pair of stone pillars. Now they were clanking up an extremely steep and twisting drive, climbing on the very mountain itself before finally drawing to a stop outside a vast edifice.

'Our humble abode,' the director said, and helped Lizbeth out.

She shivered in the icy air, then breathed in several gulps of it before looking around her. The hotel was larger than she had anticipated and all the rooms seemed to have covered balconies. Lights showed everywhere and from somewhere came the sound of a band playing a slightly old-fashioned dance tune. She glanced behind her at the way they had come, but it was too dark to see the twisting road and she went through the revolving doors into the foyer. Half the crew were crowding around the reception desk and their luggage had already been disgorged and was waiting to be taken up to their respective rooms.

'We're on the same floor,' Don said happily as Lizbeth was finally given her key and he checked the number of her room against his own. 'Almost communicating too.'

'Almost,' she replied in such a dry tone that he wagged his finger at her.

'I was only thinking of it in terms of protecting you!'

'Such protection I can do without!' She was still laughing when she saw Danny and Jackie come towards her.

'Jackie will be dining in her suite this evening,' he said. 'I suggest you come along after dinner and discuss the publicity you have arranged for her.'

'I haven't arranged anything at all. I wasn't able to fly out in advance, so I'll have to work off the cuff.'

'There was no reason why you couldn't have come here a few days ahead of time,' he said curtly.

'Except for the fact that the trip was brought forward with hardly any warning. Because of Miss Elton,' she added sharply.

'You must have *some* idea of what you're going to do,' he continued, 'or are you just going to wait around for something to happen?'

'Please,' she said in a low and angry voice. 'Let me look after my business and you look after Miss Elton. That's what you're here for, isn't it? To keep our star happy?'

His jaw set tightly and she was aware of its pugnacious thrust. 'Be careful what you say to me, Lizbeth.' His voice was equally low and angry, but she was beyond caring and spun blindly round for Don, for the second time that day using him as her safety valve.

'Come along, darling,' she said loudly. 'Let's go to our room.'

Together they went up to the first floor. Here it was slightly less hot though the heat in her bedroom itself was overpowering, the large radiator too hot to touch. She opened the window and kept it that way until the room had cooled. Then she closed it and started to unpack. The bedroom was charming, with bright rugs on the pine floor and a huge white eiderdown on the large bed. There was a capacious wardrobe and drawers and a white-tiled bathroom, with water so hot that it steamed as it left the taps.

She had agreed to meet Don downstairs for a drink at eight and she was glad they would be dining at a communal table, for it meant she would not need to entertain him. Deciding to rest before changing, she lay on the cool sheets and tried not to think of Danny and Jackie. But her thoughts played her traitor and all too easily she envisaged them together. Was his room on a different floor or did they have a communicating suite? She did not know how the Swiss regarded lovers and decided in any event that film stars made their own rules.

It was strange to think she and Danny would be sleeping under the same roof tonight, possibly only separated by a few yards. His room might even be directly above her own. Footsteps above her head set her sitting up, her pulses racing so fast that she could not help laughing at her foolishness. For one dreadful moment she had thought he might drop from the ceiling above. With a sigh she pushed aside the eiderdown and began to dress.

The black chiffon dress through which her shoulders and arms gleamed with the lustre of a pearl was a fantastic morale-booster, and confident that she looked her best, she went downstairs.

'Wow!' Don exclaimed as she came into the bar. 'You look absolutely stunning.'

She smiled her pleasure and he led her over to a table and ordered their drinks. They only had a few moments alone before the director, Jack Donald, joined them, followed by his assistant. As always when there were film people around, talk centred on the entertainment industry, with gossip about its personalities and the inevitable discussion on the state of its finances.

At eight-thirty they went in to dinner and sat around a large table. The dining-room was brightly lit and made no pretence of intimacy, but the food was excellent and of a far higher standard than that found in a British resort.

'It's a good thing we'll be taking packed lunches with us each day,' Jack said when they returned to the bar for coffee, 'otherwise we'd never get any work done in the afternoon.'

'What exactly is your schedule?' she asked. 'Hugh Edwards sent me the details, but I believe you've changed things around.'

Jack launched into an account of his plan for shooting in the coming week, and Lizbeth admired the way he had tried to minimise any hold-ups due to weather.

'We've hired a sensational house a couple of miles outside Arosa,' he continued, 'and most of the scenes will be shot there. It's supposed to be Catherine's weekend lodge, and providing the snow holds we should be able to do all our outdoor scenes in its grounds.'

'And if the snow doesn't hold?'

'Then we'll go higher up the mountains and look for it!' He glanced at his watch. 'I'm going down to the village to meet the train. Nita will be on it,' he explained.

'Nita?'

'The hairdresser from Paris. My girl-friend. It isn't only Danny Ferguson who's going to enjoy himself this trip!' He glanced from her to Don and, as she sensed the implication, her head tilted sharply.

'That makes only two of you,' she said clearly. 'Don't get any ideas about me and Don.'

'Sorry,' he said swiftly, and cuffed Don's shoulders. 'Hide the love-light, boyo, the lady doesn't like it!'

'Sorry about that,' Don said when they were alone. 'But everyone knows how I feel about you.' His eyes softened, making her conscious that quite a few people were smiling at them and enjoying the sight of the small black-haired girl and the tall, blond giant beside her.

'I'm so proud of you I could burst,' Don murmured.

Affection and exasperation warred within her, but before either emotion could win she remembered she was due to go and see Jackie. Bidding Don goodnight and averring she would be with the star for several hours, she took the lift to the second floor and the large corner suite which Jackie occupied.

It was opulently furnished and massed with flowers. Jackie and Danny were still seated at a table by the window and Lizbeth apologised for interrupting their meal.

'We're at the coffee stage,' Jackie said. 'Come and join us.'

The star drifted over to the settee, looking glamorously déshabillé in a hostess gown of lace and frills, low-cut to reveal her full breasts. Her rich dark red hair was loose around her shoulders and Lizbeth felt a pang at the sight of such voluptuous beauty. No wonder Danny desired her! Although she had not yet looked at him, her first quick glance had told her he was wearing slacks and a sweater: a white silky sweater that made his hair and brows look blacker than ever.

'I think all the photographs of me should be taken only when I'm playing the part of Catherine.' Jackie got down to business immediately. 'After all, we want to publicise the film itself and this is the first costume part I've ever played. I have a fantastic-looking wig.'

'I thought you weren't going to wear one,' Lizbeth said.

'Danny's persuaded me to change my mind.' Jackie smiled at him mistily. 'I've never known a man so able to get his own way.'

'Would you like me to arrange some publicity for you, Mr Ferguson?' Lizbeth asked, turning in his direction but refusing to meet his eyes.

'Not unless you want me to strangle you,' he said pleasantly.

Startled, she stared at him. His eyes, so clear a grey that they looked silver, stared back at her, their expression unreadable.

'I was only checking,' she said stiffly.

'Danny's here for private reasons,' Jackie purred, and crossed over to sit on the arm of his chair. 'He still finds it difficult to accept the fact that I'm news wherever I go.'

'I don't find it difficult at all,' he assured her, 'but I don't want to be part of your news.'

'Most men would give their eye teeth to be photographed with me.' The blue eyes sparkled. 'But then you aren't most men, are you? If you were, I wouldn't love you.'

Lizbeth moved abruptly and Danny saw it. 'Be careful, Jackie,' he warned. 'You're embarrassing Lizbeth.'

'Don't be silly, darling, she's not a nun.' Jackie settled back on the settee and patted the cushion beside her.

Danny ignored the gesture and rose to pour himself another cup of coffee. Lizbeth watched them both and was racking her brains what to say when there was a knock at the door and Flora Sparrow came in.

'I'd like to check the costumes with you, Miss Elton,' she said. 'If there are any alterations I can do them straight away.'

'The dresses fitted me perfectly when I tried them on in London.'

'You've had them made tighter since then,' the wardrobe mistress replied, 'and the last time you did that, we had to let out the seams again.'

'Can't it wait until tomorrow?'

'It won't take long,' Danny said gently, 'and Mrs Sparrow wants to make sure you look your most beautiful.'

With a murmur of protest, Jackie threw Danny a melting look before following Flora from the room.

Lizbeth decided to take the opportunity of escaping too, but she had reckoned without Danny who, for some obscure reason, was determined to make her stay. It was as if he enjoyed her discomfiture, for he must surely know that seeing him with Jackie was an irritant, to say the least. Indeed, his next words confirmed it.

'Do you object to my friendship with Jackie on

moral grounds,' he asked, 'or are you just plain jealous?'

'That is an uncalled-for remark!' she flared.

'Which one do you mean? The morality or the jealousy?'

'Both. I don't give a darn what you two do, and I'm certainly not jealous.'

'But you don't like Jackie?'

'Beautiful women are rarely liked by other women.'

'You aren't the type to dislike a woman because she's more beautiful than you are.' He rubbed his cheek. 'Anyway, she isn't. You're far lovelier.'

Unexpectedly tears came into her eyes. 'I do wish you wouldn't tease me,' she said tremulously.

'I'm not.' He leaned towards her. 'What have I said to make you cry?'

'Nothing.' Her tears fell faster. 'Please let me go. I'm tired.'

'Is that why you're crying?'

She nodded, and to her relief he accepted her reason. She was at the door when he called her name and she turned and looked at him.

'Are you serious about Don?'

'Why do you ask?'

'Because I want to know—and unlike you, I don't jump to conclusions. That's why I'm asking you to tell me.'

'I haven't made up my mind yet.'

'Let me know when you do.'

'So that you can put me in your little black book?'

'Watch your tongue and go to bed,' he said, not unkindly. 'Sleep well, Lizbeth, and mind you sleep alone.'

'I could say the same to you,' she retorted, 'but I won't.'

'You just have!' he said, and his chuckle followed her as she turned and fled down the corridor.

CHAPTER TEN

As Jack Donald had said, the house chosen as Catherine's lodge was fantastic. It was the home of an Argentinian meat baron, and its availability came from Jackie, who at one time had been romantically linked with him.

The first day's shooting was fraught with problems. Some of the equipment did not work in the altitude; there were several electrical breakdowns and Jackie developed a sinus condition which she threatened to relieve by having hysterics. Lizbeth could not help admiring the way Danny coped with her and wondered how they would have fared without him. He brought in a doctor from a local sanatorium who prescribed suitable medicaments to relieve the stuffy nose, but did it with such solemnity that Jackie was cajoled into believing his brilliance was saving her from a dire malady.

'Women of that temperament,' the doctor assured Lizbeth *sotto voce*, 'do not believe they ever have such a thing as the common cold—or the common anything—it must always be a mysterious virus.'

'I go along with *that*,' Lizbeth laughed. 'After all, the public pay for glamour—not a stuffy nose!'

'What were you and the doctor joking about?' Danny asked, sauntering over to her.

Without expression she told him, but he made no comment other than to shrug. It seemed she could not get under his skin no matter how hard she tried, and with some dejection she decided he was impervious to what she thought of him. If only she were equally impervious to him! But unfortunately she wasn't, and in the ensuing days she used Don as a buffer, feeling terribly guilty about it but not knowing how else she could hide her true feelings.

During most of the time when they were shooting Danny remained at the hotel, and from the clerk at Reception Lizbeth learned he was in constant touch with London and working with a secretary who had flown out to join him the day after his arrival. His week here was not the holiday he wanted people to believe it was, and it made her realise how deeply he must desire Jackie if he went to such trouble to be with her. Late each afternoon he came to collect her and most evenings they dined alone, coming down about nine-thirty to take a carriage to one or other of the hotels where they would dance or join friends—Danny appeared to know people everywhere—before returning to the hotel at midnight. Several times Lizbeth was in the lounge with Don when they came back and Jackie was always animated and laughing, happiness making her look infinitely desirable.

'A couple of the boys are taking bets on when they'll be getting married,' Don said one evening. 'I think it will be as soon as this film is finished.'

'Are you also taking bets on how long it will last?'

'That's a very cynical question.'

'I don't see why. Obviously it won't last long.'

'Why not? She's beautiful and he's rich. What can be a better combination for a happy marriage than that?'

'I know men are victims of their passions,' Lizbeth

snapped, 'but surely sex alone will pall!'

'Why should it?'

'Because Danny's too intelligent to be happy with an egomaniac.'

'Egomaniacs aren't fools,' Don cautioned, 'and Jackie's not as dumb as she makes out. After all, look at the way she's got Danny running after her.'

Lizbeth admitted the truth of this, and miserably concluded that the marriage might not be the disaster she had envisaged. From Jackie's point of view it had everything to commend it, giving her a handsome escort and sufficient financial security to satisfy even her own demanding needs. As if her very thoughts had conjured up the girl, Jackie came walking towards her. The lounge was nearly deserted and only a few people watched the star's progress.

'I hope I'm not disturbing you both?' she beamed at Don, including Lizbeth in it as if by second thoughts. 'But I'm too restless to sleep. I always get nervous when I'm filming.'

'You don't show it,' said Don. 'You're a professional to your fingertips.'

'How sweet of you to say so. But you're a sweet boy, Don, and you'll go far.'

He reddened. 'Do you honestly think so?'

Jackie nodded. 'You're a good actor and you're extremely handsome. Women always love blond men.'

'I want to appeal to them as an actor—not a male model!'

'Appeal to them in any way you can,' Jackie said bluntly. 'After all, that's an actor's duty. Find out what the public want and give it to them.'

Lizbeth appreciated the logic and conceded that Jackie was no fool.

'Take me,' the star went on. 'The men want me to be dumb and the women want to hate me for being beautiful. You can't say I let their expectations down!'

'Aren't you worried that the women will dislike you so much that it will affect you at the box office?' Lizbeth questioned.

'Not as long as their dislike is full of envy. They hate me, but they want to copy everything I do.' Scarlet nails fluttered. 'Believe me, I know what envy can do to you. I grew up in a Glasgow slum. I was thin as a pin and I had buck teeth, but I made up my mind I'd be as beautiful as Monroe. She was my idol when I was a kid.'

'I can't believe you were plain,' Don protested.

'It's true, and a good thing too. If I'd been beautiful I'd probably have been assaulted before I was ten!' Jackie shrugged. 'When you come from that sort of background you either go under or you fight. I fought.'

'And you've come to the top,' said Lizbeth, liking Jackie's honesty and wishing she didn't.

'How long will I stay there?' Jackie demanded. 'My beauty may be out of fashion next year.'

'Never,' Don asserted gallantly. 'You have a wonderful bone structure and a great reputation as an actress.'

'I love you for that,' Jackie smiled. 'I bloom on admiration.'

'Don't we all,' Lizbeth added.

'Me more than most,' Jackie said. 'I need people

as much as I need possessions. But at least I recognise my need and feed it.'

'What happens if you lose a possession?' Don asked.

Jackie's eyes went past him to rest on Lizbeth. 'Up until now I've always got what I wanted and kept it for as long as I wanted.'

'I'm sure you'll go on that way for a long time,' Lizbeth said steadily and, glancing over the girl's shoulder, saw Danny approaching. In tightly fitting black ski pants and sweater he seemed to her fevered imagination like the devil, and was even more dark by comparison with Don's blondness.

Jackie seemed to notice it too, for she stretched out her hands and placed one on each man. 'Night and day. If I ever decide to have two men at a time you'd both be ideal.'

With a silvery laugh she pulled Danny down to join her on the settee, and Lizbeth, unable to face the prospect of making conversation, rose and announced she was going to bed.

'Wait for me.' Don rose and put his hand on her arm, keeping it there until they had climbed the stairs to the first floor. Only then did he withdraw it, making it an obvious gesture. 'He fancies you, you know.'

'Who fancies whom?' she asked, annoyed by the proprietorial air he had managed to create between them when they had left the lounge. No matter that she had tried to create it many times herself, Don had no business to do it.

'Danny Ferguson, of course. I saw the way he was watching you.'

'You're mad! He dotes on Jackie. A little while

ago you said you thought they'd be getting married soon.'

'I said it but I didn't believe it. I was testing you.'

Her hands clenched. 'What is that supposed to mean? If you're implying that I want Danny for myself . . .'

'He's got everything going for him,' Don said stubbornly, 'and you're always tensed up when he's around.'

'Because I can't stand him! I hate him,' she cried, 'can't you get that into your head?'

'I wish I could.' He paused and stared deep into her eyes. 'But he does fancy you, Liz. I've seen the way he looks at you.'

'Me and a hundred others!' She quickened her pace and reached her door. 'Goodnight, Don. I'll see you in the morning.'

'Are you mad at me?' he asked miserably. 'But I love you so much I——'

'I'm not mad at you,' she said wearily. 'But I'd like you to curb your imagination.'

'I'll try.' He caught her hand. 'Let me kiss you, Lizbeth. I need you so much.'

But this was more than she could tolerate. 'Not tonight, Don. I'm not in the mood for kisses—not even Danny's!'

'I deserved that,' he said so miserably that contrition almost made her accede to his request. Then she controlled her weakness and stepped quickly into her bedroom.

For the first time the next morning, the main shooting was delayed by bad weather and Jack Donald decided to get in some extra footage on a chase scene, which left the main leads free for the day.

'Let's go for a walk,' Don suggested to Lizbeth, happy again now that she had had breakfast with him and assured him she was not angry about last night.

It was better than sitting around the hotel and being asked to keep Jackie company if Danny was working, so she nodded, said she had some news to type out first, and then joined Don outside the hotel at noon.

The sky seemed to have grown darker, but he told her he had checked with the clerk who had said there was no likelihood of a storm.

'I still don't want to go too far from the hotel,' she said.

'You're chicken,' he teased. 'I want to take you up in the ski lift.'

'On a day like this?'

'Why not? It's still going, and there's a little restaurant at the top of the mountain that's famous for its food. We can have a spot of lunch there and then come down again.'

'It would be much nicer to go when it's sunny.'

'When it's sunny, I'm filming,' he said reasonably, 'and when the filming's over we fly home. Have a heart, Lizbeth, this is the only free time I'm likely to have.'

It seemed churlish to refuse and she accompanied him to the ski lift. There were none of the usual crowds outside and she hoped it was not working. But the ticket collector took their money and gave them tickets, strapped them into the bucket chairs and wished them a cheery goodbye.

Lizbeth gripped the sides of the wooden seat. The attendant had wrapped a rug around her and though she was not cold she felt the wind icy on her face. Slowly the chair moved along the steel cable and soon she saw the village set out below her. Even in the greyness it was a picturesque sight: the steep pitched roofs, white with snow, and the chalets themselves gleaming brown and orange and other varied colours. The railway station was misted over and she turned and glanced above to where the top of the ski lift could be seen hundreds of yards away. Slowly it drew nearer and Don, reaching the end of the line first, stood free and ready to help her as she came near him.

'I thought there was an attendant here?' she asked.

'Maybe he thought the ski lift was closing,' Don said and, catching her by the hand, trudged with her up the incline to the hut. He opened the door and they went in. It was deserted and he called out and then went round the counter.

Lizbeth joined him and saw a sheet of paper set half under a plate. There was German writing on it and she picked it up and tried to decipher it. Her German was rusty but sufficient for her to understand what she was reading.

'Weather report bad and returning to village. We have left hut unlocked in case any skiers come down from the higher slopes. There is food in the refrigerator. Check the cost of it against the menu and please leave payment on the counter. Heidi Gottfried.'

'Well, that's clear enough,' said Don. 'At least we can make ourselves something to eat, and having promised you——'

'I'd rather get back down again before the ski lift stops,' Lizbeth interrupted, and not waiting for Don to answer, ran out of the hut and down the slope, her feet, in their ski boots, slithering on the ice. The sky had grown considerably darker and snowflakes were swirling down. So much for the clerk's assertion that there would not be a storm. From the look of the clouds the weather was more likely to get worse than better. Annoyed with Don and even more annoyed with herself for letting him talk her into coming up here, she quickened her pace, ignoring his call as he tried to catch up with her. Ahead was the entrance to the ski lift and she hurried towards the small kiosk that housed the attendant.

Dismayed, she saw it was empty, as was the whole shed which housed the cables and machinery. Worse still, it was totally silent, with no reassuring hum coming from the generators, nor a clickety-clack from the ski lift as chairs came slowly up the mountain side.

'It's shut,' she called as Don reached her side. 'That's why there was no attendant here when we arrived. We must have been the last two people to come up.'

'It looks as if you're right.' Don walked the length of the small platform, peered at the huge cable drum, now motionless, and several bucket chairs hanging disconsolately from a suspended steel cable.

'Why didn't they warn us?' Lizbeth asked angrily. 'They had no business letting us come up here if they knew they would be closing.'

'Looks as if they slipped up.'

'They'll have a bit of explaining to do when I get

down again!' Lizbeth's anger grew. 'What do we do now? We can't stay here.'

'We've got no choice.' He stamped his feet and flailed himself with his arms. 'Let's get back to the hut, Lizbeth. At least we'll be warm there.'

'But we can't stay in the hut. We've got to get down to Arosa.'

'The only way is to ski down. The attendant probably thought that was what we were going to do. That's why he must have let us come up.'

'Surely he saw we had no skis with us?' She walked out of the hut and a few yards up the incline to peer at the track down which skiers usually began their descent. From what she could see of it, it looked smooth though steep. 'The only thing we can do is to walk down,' she muttered.

'And get stuck in a snowdrift? Don't be crazy. The snow looks hard, but we'd be taking a hell of a risk if we tried to walk on it. There's only one thing to do. Get back to the hut and wait there until the weather clears.'

'According to you it shouldn't have got worse.' He coloured and she saw it. 'You made it up,' she accused. 'You lied about what the clerk said.'

'I didn't lie,' he protested. 'I was just a bit more optimistic than he was.'

'How much more optimistic? Tell me the truth, Don. You've got us stuck up here, so there's no point not being honest.'

'The clerk said it might snow a bit, but he definitely didn't say the weather was going to close in completely.'

He glanced around disconsolately. The village was completely hidden by a thick blanket of grey mist which, even as they watched it, began to obliterate hillocks and trees, rising higher and higher until Lizbeth had the impression she was standing on a cloud in the very centre of the sky itself. Even the hut was fast disappearing and, afraid they might lose their bearings, she turned and climbed up the path.

'We would have been in a fine pickle if the hut had been locked.' She made no attempt to hide her fury and Don, guiltily aware that he was the cause of it, remained silent.

Once they were inside the hut some of Lizbeth's anger abated. The dynamo which supplied electricity was still working, which meant there was both light and heat here, and since there also seemed to be a plentiful supply of food they would at least be warm and comfortable until the ski lift started working again.

'I supose we'd better make the best of it,' she said. 'What will you have, Don—coffee or chocolate?'

'Chocolate, but I'll make it for us.'

He proceeded to do so and she went to a table and sat down. There was no point looking through the window, for there was nothing to see but swirling white mist, and it was somehow frightening to know they were suspended here, as invisible to others as others were invisible to them.

'How long do you think it will last?' she asked as Don brought two steaming cups of chocolate over to the table.

'The clerk said this kind of weather clears up at night when the wind comes.'

'What happens if it doesn't come?'

'Then we could be stuck here until tomorrow.'

'Or even longer,' she said sombrely. 'Someone in

the hotel was saying that when they were here last year the ski lift was closed for three days because of the mists.'

'I'm sure it won't be as bad as that.'

Don's look was far less cheerful than his words and she knew her comment had shaken him. But he deserved to be shaken, for it was his childish stupidity that had put them in this position. Still, there was nothing she could do about it and to go on being angry would serve no purpose. She took off her anorak and sipped her chocolate. At best they would have four or five hours here. At worst they could be here overnight and, at the very worst, several days. She shied away from this last thought. Time enough to think of that when it happened.

The hours slowly passed. There was no change in the colour of the scene outside—it remained a pale grey blanket of mist—and only her hunger made her aware that the day was slowly moving on. There was a large pile of magazines on a table in the corner and she and Don leafed through them until he found a pack of cards and taught her how to play three-column gin rummy. But after two hours of playing, even this game palled and she was glad when hunger became sufficiently strong for them to break the monotony by preparing a meal. Luckily there was a mound of sausages in the refrigerator as well as a bowl of eggs and some slices of pink succulent ham.

Soon an appetising aroma of food wafted around the hut and Don searched out crockery and cutlery and set them on a table nearest the counter. Then he prowled around looking into the cupboard and finally emerged from one with a triumphant look on his face.

'Found it!' he said, and held aloft a bottle of brandy. 'I knew they were bound to have some of this up here just in case there was an accident. Unfortunately there's no wine.'

Lizbeth echoed this sentiment as she saw Don pour himself what she considered to be an over-generous measure of brandy, but she knew better than to comment on it. If she did, bravado could well make him tip the bottle again, but she was resolute in refusing to have a drink herself and was quick to make two large cups of coffee to set on the table at the same time as she set out the food.

'It's a bit like being marooned on a desert island with all mod. cons.,' said Don, cutting a sausage and dipping it into a creamy egg yolk.

'I'm glad you're enjoying it,' she said dryly.

'Aren't you?' He glanced up and saw her expression. 'Come on, Lizbeth, nothing is going to happen to us here. I admit it was stupid of me to bring you, but it was *only* stupid. You're acting as if I've been criminally negligent.'

She could not in all honesty say that she thought he was, merely that he had behaved thoughtlessly, but as she had already said this it was pointless to reiterate it, and instead she reached for the coffee pot to replenish their cups.

'Not for me,' Don said. 'I prefer the brandy.' He sipped it appreciatively and then helped himself to some more sausages. Afterwards he helped her to clear the table, but because they were not sure about the adequacy of the water supply, they decided not to wash up and instead stacked everything in the sink.

It was now half-past four and the mist had darkened appreciably, making it necessary for them to switch on the lights. The radiators were still working and the hut was warm. Underneath the counter Don found a transistor radio and soon the strains of a Viennese waltz filled their ears. Within a few moments it was interrupted by the voice of an announcer giving the latest state of the weather.

Lizbeth listened, her sense of calm disappearing as she faced the fact that she and Don looked like being marooned up here for the rest of the day and evening. Indeed they would be lucky if they were able to get down to Arosa tomorrow.

'It's a good job all the indoor shooting has been done,' she told him, 'otherwise they'd have your scalp.'

'Don't remind me.' Don wandered over to the window and peered out. 'I wonder what the rest of the unit are doing?'

'Wondering what's happened to us,' she said wryly. 'I don't suppose you thought to tell anyone where we were going?'

'The clerk knows.' Don came back to sit opposite her. 'I don't suppose they'll send up a rescue party, though. I mean, they'll know we're in this hut so they won't want to risk anyone's life and have them climb up the mountain in the dark.'

'For two pins I would try and climb down.'

'Luckily I don't have two pins,' Don said at once, 'and I wouldn't let you risk your neck anyway.' His head tilted. 'It's far too lovely a neck.'

She shied away from his tone. The last thing in

the world she wanted was for Don to get romantic now, several thousand feet up a remote mountain and marooned in a world of snow and mist. 'Talking of necks, I'd still like to wring yours,' she said bracingly. 'This will be the last time I'll take *your* word on anything.'

'At least up here you're spared from being at Jackie Elton's beck and call.'

'She has Danny,' Lizbeth replied, keeping her voice casual.

'Roped but not tied and still giving the occasional kick—as I said last night.'

'Don't start that again,' she warned.

'Sorry.' Don eyed her. 'You have no reason to dislike him, have you? He didn't make a pass at you, did he?'

'Every time we meet he makes a pass at me,' she said brightly, deciding on a new approach. 'After all, he's so ugly and poor and stupid that he can't get any girl to look at him.'

Don laughed and slid his chair across the floor to a stop next to hers. They were so close that their knees were touching and he put up his hand and rubbed her cheek.

'Your skin is pink and your eyes are gleaming like stars,' he whispered. 'You have a changing beauty, Lizbeth. Just when I think I know your face I find I don't know it at all.' His voice lowered. 'Like now, for instance, when you look like a little girl and last night when you looked so sexy and provocative.'

'And tomorrow when I'll have a stuffy nose and red eyes,' she quipped. 'Or haven't you noticed that it's getting colder in here?'

With an exclamation Don jumped up and went to put his hand on the radiator. 'You're right, it's cooler. I wonder if the generator has given out.'

'Perhaps it works on a time switch?'

He shook his head. 'The lights are still working.'

As if his words were a signal, the lights went out. There was a short silence, then Lizbeth laughed. 'You're no genie, Don. You'd better watch your words from now on.'

He snorted and she heard his steps across the floor boards. 'When I was looking for the brandy I noticed a hurricane lamp in one of the cupboards. Let's hope I can remember which one it was in.' There was a muffled oath as he knocked against a chair, then a door creaked. 'Got it,' he said. 'Let's hope it's full of paraffin.'

Lizbeth remained where she was, realising how miserable it was going to be if they had to face darkness as well as cold, but hardly had this come into her mind when a pale lemon glow illuminated the room and Don came triumphantly towards her, brandishing a brass lamp.

'I won't turn the wick full up,' he said, 'because I don't know how long this will have to last us.'

'We needn't keep it on the whole time,' she replied. 'Just occasionally to stop us getting morbid.'

'I'm sorry about all this, Lizbeth. I had no idea things were going to work out this way. But the thought of being alone with you was too good a chance for me to miss.'

'Being alone with you won't make me change my mind about you, Don.'

'I won't give up hoping.'

She pointed to the lamp. 'How about turning it

off for a while? It will be better to have it on when we're feeling cold.'

'I'll see if I can find any blankets.'

Together they searched the room and underneath a wooden seat found a pile of rugs. 'At least this will help to soften the floor,' Don remarked.

'Do you think we'll be here all night?'

'It looks like it. The mist has completely closed in.'

She shivered. 'I hope no one's worrying about us. You're sure you did tell the clerk where we were going?'

'Positive.' He stamped his feet. 'It's amazing how quickly it gets cold when the heating goes.'

'What about some supper? I'm afraid it will have to be the same as we had before.'

'It suits me fine.' He went with her to the counter. 'It's a good thing Heidi cooks on calor gas and not electricity.'

'I'm glad you can see the bright side of things.'

Don grinned. 'It could be worse. I mean, the hut could have been closed.'

'Don't talk about it,' she pleaded. 'We might have frozen to death.'

'I know.' His tone was sober and he seemed to appreciate the enormity of their luck and his own foolhardiness at not seeing how disastrous their trip could have turned out if Heidi Gottfried had locked the hut before she returned to Arosa.

'Mind you, you could always have broken the door down,' Lizbeth reassured him.

'Just because you see the hero do it in a film it doesn't mean it's easy,' Don quipped. 'This door is made of stout planks, not balsa wood!'

She laughed. 'It would certainly have spoilt your image for me to see you banging on the door and failing to break it down. You wouldn't have been my hero any more.'

'I've never been your hero,' he said shortly.

His anger was sudden, and afraid to arouse it further she gave him some eggs to break into a bowl, hoping that having something to do would distract him.

'We'll have omelettes,' she said, 'and save the sausages for the morning.'

Supper was a less cheerful meal than lunch, for they both knew they were likely to be here for the rest of the night and possibly the following day. The hut was cold and as soon as they had eaten Don piled the rugs on to the floor, making as thick a mound as possible, though keeping several to use as covers. Lizbeth settled herself on them, tensing as Don did the same.

'Don't be scared of me,' he said abruptly. 'But we'll be warmer if we lie close together.'

'I'm not scared,' she denied, and forced herself not to stiffen as he pulled her into the circle of his arms. But his hold remained passive and after a moment she relaxed. It was certainly warmer with the rugs over them and though it was not the most comfortable of beds it was not as hard as she had expected.

'It's going to be a very long night,' she whispered. 'It's only eight o'clock.'

'How about a brandy? It might help you to sleep.'

'No, thanks.'

She spoke so quickly that he laughed. 'Do you

think I'll get drunk and forget my honourable intentions?'

'Yes,' she said candidly, 'I do.'

'Then I won't have any brandy. As I've already scared you half to death the least I can do is to reassure you now.' The humour of his words eased her mind as no fervid declaration could have done, and she closed her eyes.

'Let's recite Shakespeare,' Don suggested. 'That's a good way of passing the time.'

'You'll be better at it than me.'

'Well, I'll stick to Shakespeare and you can bring in the poets too.'

'That's better,' she agreed, and immediately launched into *Hiawatha*. When she stopped, Don started on *The Merchant of Venice*, quoting Antonio and Portia as well as Shylock and Bassanio. He had a melodious voice and it was a pleasure to hear him.

'I feel as if I'm listening to the radio,' she whispered when, after some twenty minutes, he paused for breath. 'I bet you know the whole play.'

'Near enough,' he admitted. 'Every drama student acts in it at one time or another. I know *Julius Caesar* and a good bit of *Henry V* too.'

'Once more unto the breach, dear friends,' she quoted, 'or close the wall up with our English dead.'

He laughed and pulled her head down to rest on his shoulder. 'The very least I can do is to offer myself as a pillow.'

'I'm sure there's a fitting quotation for that,' she responded, 'but I can't think of one.'

'I can think of several, but they'd get me a slap on the face!'

'Go back to Venice,' she ordered.

'Back to Venice it shall be.'

Don's voice began to recite softly in her ears. It was lighter than Danny's; a golden voice and not a dark brown one. Dear heaven, why did she have to think of Danny at this moment? Was it because she knew that had she been here with him instead of Don, she would be feeling and behaving quite differently? Her cheeks burned and with an incoherent murmur she burrowed her face into the rough pile of a rug.

'Relax,' Don whispered. 'It won't go on for ever. We'll soon be safe.'

Lizbeth was glad he did not know how ironic his remark was. Yes, she would be safe once she was out of Danny's life. Safe and unhappy. Her lids lowered, fluttered, and she slept.

CHAPTER ELEVEN

LIZBETH opened her eyes to moonlight and, lying on the pile of rugs on the floor, was able to look through the window panes to see a star-studded sky.

'Don!' she cried. 'The mist has gone.'

Don grunted and sat up, then jumped to his feet and went over to the window, shivering in the cold air. 'It's a perfect night,' he murmured. 'Come and have a look.'

Wrapping a rug around her, she did so. The mountains were so clear she felt she could put out her hand and touch them. They glinted silver blue in the light of the moon, while the trees that ranged the slopes to the left looked like black sentinels.

'Do you think they'll be starting the lift?' she asked.

'I'll go and see.'

Zipping himself into his jacket, he went out, and Lizbeth started to make some coffee. Apart from the sounds of her own movements it was as quiet as the grave up here, but it was the quietness of calm and she had no fear of being left alone.

The coffee was percolating by the time Don returned, and one look at his face told her he had good news. 'I found a bell in the hut that communicates with the ski lift at the bottom of the mountain. I put my finger on it and didn't take it off until someone replied. I couldn't talk to them, of course, but at least they'll realise there's someone stuck up here waiting to get down. They'll probably start the lift as soon as it's light.'

'Let's have some coffee and then go and see if anything is happening.'

A few moments later they set off. The stars were fading and the sky was getting lighter, though it was still not yet dawn. It was bitterly cold and within seconds Lizbeth's face was numb. But she was too keyed up to feel any discomfort and she steadied herself against Don as they crunched their way down the incline. Even before they reached the little shed they heard the whine of the cable.

'It's working,' Don said excitedly. 'Just before we take the chairs I'll give them a buzz on the bell to let them know we're on our way down.'

'You don't think the lift will suddenly stop?' she asked anxiously. 'I don't fancy being marooned in a cable car.'

'Don't worry about that. Now it's started, they won't stop till we're safely below.'

Trying to let his words reassure her, she fastened herself into a bucket chair, her eyes straining ahead as she began to descend. It was eerie to be the only moving figure in a silent landscape, particularly when one was poised hundreds of feet above it. How large and bare the mountains were, their crags and boulders smoothed by a thick shroud of snow. She glanced over her shoulder and saw Don following behind. He waved and she took her hand away from the arm of the chair and waved back, then clung to the side again as the chair swung beneath her twisting body. Silently they glided down, the pace occasionally slowing and making her tense with fear lest they stop altogether, but the movements did not cease and soon she was able to relax and think with pleasure of the warmth of the hotel and the comfort of her own bed. Not that she would have any chance of sleeping in it, for it was now dawn and looked like being a bright day. Jack would be filming the outside scenes and she would have to be there with the photographer to get as many shots of Jackie and Don as possible.

Ahead of her she saw the entrance to the ski lift and could make out a group of people waiting. She leaned forward and her chair rocked so that she forced herself to lie back in it until the ground was only a couple of feet below her. An elderly man in uniform stretched out to grasp the chair, steadying it as he undid the straps that had tied her in. Stiffly she stood up and moved forward, recognising Jack and Danny as well as several of the camera crew and some unknown Swiss.

'Thank goodness you're safe!' Jack exclaimed. 'We've been up all night worrying about you.'

'Didn't you know we were in the hut?'

'We were pretty sure you were, but there was always an element of doubt.'

'I didn't know if Don had had the sense to stay up there.' Danny was speaking, his voice harsh. He looked harsh too, his mouth set in a thin line and his lids low over his eyes, turning them into silver slits. Stubble lay upon his cheeks and chin, accentuating his darkness. Lizbeth knew he was angry and could not help a thrill of pleasure at knowing it was caused by fear for her safety. But the pleasure evaporated as he caught her roughly by the arm and pulled her to one side.

'If you wanted to spend a night with Don, couldn't you have chosen a better place?' he snapped.

'I didn't know we'd be stuck there. You don't think we did it purposely?'

'Do you expect me to believe it was an accident? The clerk told you the weather was getting worse. If you didn't want to be marooned in the hut, why did you go there?'

'I didn't know it was going to get worse.'

'Don't lie to me!'

Unwilling to say anything that would redound to Don's discredit, she remained silent, a fact which only increased Danny's temper.

'The forecast said there was going to be a blizzard. Who did you think was going to ski in that kind of weather? You knew damn well the lift would stop!'

He was pulling her along the track as he spoke, moving so fast that they were soon several yards ahead of the group. She glanced over her shoulder and saw Don talking to Jack. She stumbled over a lump of snow and was given another vicious shake.

'Don't worry,' Danny grated, 'lover boy is right behind you!'

'He isn't my lover boy!'

'Oh yeah? What did you do all night? Play snap?'

'Gin rummy, as a matter of fact. And then we went to sleep. Sleep!' she cried. 'Don't judge Don by the way *you* would have behaved in similar circumstances!'

His fingers dug painfully into her arm. 'I'd have had more sense than to get you involved in such a stupid escapade. I suppose you know you won't be able to keep it out of the papers?'

'Since I spend my life trying to get news into the

papers,' she snapped, 'why should I try to keep this out?'

'Because you're involved in it. Not just some damn fool actor, but *you*. Or don't you care that everyone will know you spent the night alone with your boy-friend?'

'You should get someone to re-write your dialogue. You talk like something out of Noah's Ark! Just because I spent the night in a hut with Don it doesn't mean my reputation is ruined. Nor does it mean that everyone will jump to the same ridiculous conclusions as you!'

'He wants you!' Danny ground out through clenched teeth. 'That's why he took you to the hut. So don't expect me to believe he didn't have you.'

'I don't expect you to believe anything.' She almost screamed the words at him. 'And I don't care what you believe! I care nothing for you or your opinions, Danny Ferguson, and the sooner you get out of my life the better!'

'That goes for me too.' He dropped her arm as though it were a piece of hot coal and strode on ahead of her. She stopped walking and waited for Don and the others to catch up with her.

'I'll be fine after I've had a hot bath,' Don was saying to Jack. 'And if there are any bags under my eyes it shouldn't matter too much. After all, I'm supposed to be Catherine's lover!'

In the blue light of dawn Jack's teeth flashed white as he grinned from Don to Lizbeth.

'Don't you start with your innuendoes,' she flared. 'I've had quite enough from Danny!'

'He was worried about you,' Jack replied. 'It was several hours before we actually knew for sure that you were at the hut. The reception clerk had gone off duty and the one who took over from him didn't know where you were. It wasn't until the manager rang the day clerk at ten o'clock last night that we found out.'

Lizbeth's anger partially ebbed. This explanation to some extent excused Danny's anger, which she now saw as being composed of fear for her safety, but it did not explain all the accusations he had hurled at her, and as she trudged towards the hotel she tried to analyse them. Only one reason for his behaviour came into her mind, and it was so incredible that she could not believe it. Danny was jealous of Don. She stopped so abruptly that Don knocked into her and put his arm out to steady her.

'Tired?' he asked.

'A little,' she lied, and refused to think of Danny again until she was alone and able to do so without interruption. But then, with breakfast inside her and warmth pervading her body, the thought of Danny being jealous of her made no sense whatever. It was far more likely to be pique that she preferred Don.

A knock at her door brought her swiftly to her feet, but it was Jackie Elton who came in at her call, and Lizbeth stared at her in surprise.

'I came to see if you were feeling better,' the star said. She was wearing trousers and sweater and a mink coat was slung over her shoulders. 'I'm waiting to be made up, so I thought I'd pop in and see you.'

'I'm feeling fine,' Lizbeth answered. 'It wasn't much of an ordeal. It was cold in the hut, but at least we weren't hungry.'

'And you were with Don,' Jackie said. 'That must have been a big compensation.'

Lizbeth's silky black hair swung back as she tilted her head sharply. 'Neither of us knew the ski lift was going to stop working.'

'I'm not saying you did.'

'You're hinting it.' Lizbeth was too angry to worry about offending Jackie. At this moment she was merely another girl. 'If Don and I wanted to make love, we didn't need to do it in the most public way possible. And you and Danny have no right to ...' Fury caught in her throat and choked her, intensifying as Jackie Elton smiled openly.

'Personally, I couldn't care less what you and Don do. As you say, one doesn't have to make opportunity these days, one just takes it where one likes.'

'I don't like,' Lizbeth grated. 'I'm not Don's girlfriend, and if you and Danny say one more thing to me about it I'll explode!'

'You can't blame Danny for being angry,' said Jackie. 'To begin with he was worried that you and Don might have been killed—and that would have put a hex on the film.'

'Indeed it would!'

'And then when he found out that you and Don had gone up to the hut knowing about the blizzard ——' The blue eyes sparkled with mischief. 'You make it so clear you don't like Danny that he can't bear to be cut out by another man. The poor darling is too used to having girls fall over themselves to attract him.'

'Why should he want me when he's got you?' Lizbeth snapped.

'He doesn't really want you, darling. But the fact

that *you* don't want him is rather off-putting to his ego.' Jackie gave a sigh. 'It's a good thing I can accept Danny with all his faults. But then if he wasn't a skirt-chaser he wouldn't have chased me. I'll get used to his roving eye, I suppose. At least once we're married I know he'll have to come home after each little affair.'

'It sounds an ideal marriage for the two of you,' Lizbeth said. 'I can only say that you deserve each other.'

'Thank you, darling.' Jackie went to the door. 'Danny can be so wonderful and loving when he's in the mood that I'm willing to take the rough with the smooth.'

The money and power Danny could exert on Jackie Elton's behalf was also part of the smooth, Lizbeth knew, but restrained herself from saying so. Besides, there was no point continuing the argument.

Later that morning, when she saw Jack Donald, he asked her why Jackie had come to her room.

'To see how I was,' Lizbeth told him.

'What else did she want?' Jack asked.

'What makes you think she wanted anything?'

'Jackie never wastes time talking to someone of her own sex unless there's something in it for her.'

Lizbeth pondered over this when Jack went away to round up the rest of the crew. She had been surprised when Jackie had sought her out earlier and had made such a point of explaining away Danny's behaviour at the ski lift. It was as if Jackie did not want his actions misconstrued. But if this were the case, then what exactly had motivated Danny? Once again, she was back to the word 'jealousy,' and because she longed to believe this, she was afraid to give it credence. Slowly she crossed the foyer and was halfway to the stairs when the object of her thoughts came out of the elevator. He was formally dressed in a dark suit and white shirt and, interpreting the look she gave him, said:

'I'm flying home.'

'Tired of being on location?' she asked flippantly.

'I assumed we would all be leaving today. I hadn't bargained on bad weather holding up the shooting.' He gave her a sarcastic look. 'Have you recovered from your ordeal?'

'It wasn't an ordeal.'

His eyes moved so slowly over her body that it was like an insult. Heat invaded her and she longed to lash out at him. 'It would have been an ordeal with you, Mr Ferguson, but not with Don.'

'You didn't act that way in the car with me.'

She remembered the passion between them; remembered too that he had gone from her to meet Jackie at the airport. 'It isn't only your dialogue that needs modernising—your ideas are antiquated too. Girls like sex just as much as men do, and these days they don't mind admitting it.'

'How about a weekend away with me, then?'

Head high, she looked at him. 'You don't appeal to me any more, Mr Ferguson. You're too shop-soiled.'

His face, ashen despite its swarthiness, remained in her mind for the rest of the day, even coming in front of her eyes when she finally returned to England late the following evening. No matter how provoking he had been, she should never have spoken to him like that. All she had done was to put herself on the same level as him.

Lizbeth's decision to leave her job as soon as Judy was ready to take over from her was thwarted by Danny's refusal to agree to this, a fact communicated to her by a curt note from him saying he expected her to work her full three months' notice.

Lizbeth's first instinct was to send back a rude reply, but on her way out of the office for a luncheon appointment she met him in the downstairs foyer. He was standing at the reception desk and barred her way as he saw her emerging from the elevator.

'I was going to give you a call after lunch,' he said.

'If it's about your letter——'

'It's about a press party I want you to organise for Kurt Voegler.'

Dumbfounded, she gazed at him and he smiled mockingly. 'I finally persuaded Voegler that if he's going to come out of retirement to make a film for me, he might as well go the whole way.'

'But he hates publicity.'

'He wants to open a meditation centre in Monte Carlo and I've promised that we'll do a film about it once he's got it organised.'

'A sprat to catch a mackerel,' Lizbeth remarked. 'You're lucky you have a sprat to dangle.'

'What bait do *you* bite on?' he asked.

'None that's on your line. Look elsewhere for your fun, Mr Ferguson, if Miss Elton isn't woman enough for you!'

His lids lowered, giving his face a mask-like look. With the strong but finely-chiselled features and well-shaped head he could have posed for a statue of a Greek god. 'What would you do if I said you were the only one who is woman enough for me?'

'Laugh,' she replied.

His lids rose and his eyes stared directly into hers. The subdued lighting had made the pupils dilate and the irises were just a fine silver grey rim around them. 'We don't seem to be able to have a conversation without it deteriorating into a verbal battle. Couldn't we have a truce?'

'An armed one only.' She made to walk past and he turned and walked with her to the entrance.

'Can I give you a lift?' he asked, pointing to his car and chauffeur.

She shrugged and followed him into the car, asking the driver to let her off at the Savoy. 'I'm going there too,' Danny commented. 'Do you have a business or personal lunch?'

'I don't have personal lunches during working hours,' she said shortly. 'I'm meeting J. D. Rexham.'

'The T.V. critic?'

'He's much more than that,' said Lizbeth. 'He's the most respected man in Fleet Street. If he gives anything a good review it becomes a guaranteed box office success.'

'Then we'd better make sure he likes our two new series.'

'You can't buy him,' she said crisply.

'You can encourage goodwill.' Danny's answer was equally crisp.

'That's why I'm having lunch with him,' Lizbeth said. 'And of course I'll make sure he's the first person to know that Mr. Voegler's agreed to a Press party. When is it to be, by the way?'

'Next Tuesday. I want it to be a first-class affair. Pick a private room at the Savoy and only invite the best known critics. And Jackie, of course. She'll be co-starring with Voegler, so she'll be there.'

'She's getting her photograph with him after all,' Lizbeth could not help saying, and saw Danny fling her a sharp look.

'Jackie gets what she wants provided I think it's good for N.A.T. If it weren't, she wouldn't get it.'

Lizbeth's sniff was audible, but it aroused no comment and they completed the rest of the short journey in silence.

Returning to the office after a short but successful lunch—J.D. Rexham did not believe in prolonging a meal—Lizbeth set about writing a personal letter to the small group of élite men she wanted to meet Kurt Voegler. Naturally J. D. Rexham headed the list, and this meant that a couple of other excellent critics—whom he thoroughly disliked and always refused to be seen with—could not be invited.

'I know he's considered the best in his field,' Mrs Allen remarked, 'but I still wouldn't let him dictate to me as to whom I could ask to a party.'

'I don't like it either,' Lizbeth admitted, 'but he's the tops in his profession and Mr Voegler needs the prestige of Rexham's newspaper.'

'And you really mean you can't invite Durford?'

'I daren't. Durford married J. D.'s first wife and they hate each other. Durford also pipped J. D. to a Pulitzer Prize.'

'Beats me how you remember all the gossip,' Mrs Allen grinned.

'My job depends on it,' Lizbeth said.

'Depends on what?' a voice asked, and both women looked sharply to the door to see Jackie Elton leaning against it, Mrs Allen raised an eyebrow in Lizbeth's direction—the eyebrow furthest away from Jackie—and then went out of the office.

'Who's J. D.?' Jackie asked. 'And who can't be invited to a party to meet him?'

Briefly Lizbeth explained her predicament. It was the first time she had seen Jackie since their meeting in Arosa and she smarted from the memory. But Jackie seemed to have forgotten it, or else she was a better actress than anyone had given her credit for.

'Will you be at the party too?' she asked, as Lizbeth stopped talking.

'Naturally.'

'Let one of your male assistants come instead. I want to be the only woman there.' A narrow hand raked the red hair away from the creamy-skinned forehead. 'It will make a much better story for the papers. "Jackie Elton, the only woman Kurt Voegler agrees to see when he comes out of retirement." Don't you think it sounds good?'

'I don't think you need that sort of story,' Lizbeth said casually.

'I don't want you to come,' Jackie repeated.

Lizbeth forced herself to keep calm. 'If you're telling me how to run my office——'

'Suggesting, darling, not telling you. But if you would prefer to have a word with Danny about it...'

'That won't be necessary,' said Lizbeth. There was no doubt that if Jackie put her demands to him he would agree to them, and the last thing in the world she could face was to have him give her yet another order.

'Very well,' she murmured. 'I'll play it your way.'

'I knew you would,' Jackie beamed. 'You really

are sweet, Lizbeth.'

With a wave of her hand she drifted out, and Lizbeth was forced to admire the way in which Jackie got what she wanted. All this and Danny too.

CHAPTER TWELVE

TEN letters of invitation were sent out and signed by Lizbeth, and the acceptances were unanimous and immediate. Everyone wanted to meet Kurt Voegler. Remembering her promise to Jackie not to attend, Lizbeth arranged for one of the young men from the Press Office to go instead. He would have little to do, for Danny would be there as well, and she felt she could rely on his discretion to see that no one asked Voegler questions he would find embarrassing to answer.

She half expected Danny to comment on her own absence, but he did not do so and she wondered if Jackie had told him it was at her suggestion.

On the day of the dinner she went to the private room they had booked at the Savoy and checked that all the arrangements were complete. She had chosen the food and the wine with great care, deferring to the suggestions of the *maître*, who appreciated her desire to make this dinner one to be remembered. Because she knew she would be on edge—even more so since she would not be present—she decided to spend the evening with Don. It was the first time she had agreed to see him since their return from Switzerland and he saw it as her total forgiveness of his behaviour.

'I'm glad to be with you tonight,' he said when they had reached the coffee stage of their meal, 'but I think you were crazy to let Jackie talk you out of going to the Voegler party.'

Her shrug admitted the truth of Don's comment, but she did not want to verbalise on it. A sense of foreboding had been with her for the whole of the day, though there was no rhyme or reason for it. She sipped some wine and allowed the waiter to refill her glass. By the time Don drove her home she was in a more relaxed state of mind though she refused to let him drive her past the Savoy.

'When will you know how the dinner went?' he asked as he drew up outside her flat.

'I've told my assistant to phone me as soon as he's free tonight. That's why I wanted to come home early.'

'You just wanted an excuse to get rid of me,' Don grumbled good-naturedly, 'and as it *is* early, you can't refuse to let me in for a coffee.'

Annoyed that she had fallen into a trap of her own making, she agreed to Don's suggestion, and saw him smile as he followed her up the steps.

In the flat she immediately set about making coffee while he put on some music. 'Coming home with you like this has been the best part of the evening,' he said as he took his coffee cup from her and settled with it on the settee. 'We should do this more often. Just be friends, I mean,' he added quickly. 'You might find I grow on you.'

Lizbeth smiled and wisely did not disabuse him. Once she left National Amalgamated it would be easier to slip out of Don's life, and this would be particularly the case if she went with her father to India.

As though guessing her thoughts Don asked whether her father had raised the money for his documentary film, and looked pleased when she said he had.

'If he needs any more backers, he should go and see Danny,' Don said. 'Jackie was telling me that N.A.T. are going in for documentaries in a big way.'

'I don't want any favours from Danny.'

'It wouldn't be a favour. Anyway, *you* don't need to ask him. It's something your father could do.'

Aware of Don looking at her speculatively and not liking the gleam in his eyes, she quickly stood up and held out her hand to replenish his coffee. Before she could take it, the doorbell rang, the sound so unexpected that it startled her.

'Maybe it's your assistant,' Don said, and went to answer it.

Lizbeth followed him and as she reached the hall, Don opened the front door, falling back a step as a tall, wide-shouldered figure pushed its way in. Astonishment kept her where she was and Danny strode over to her. He was blazing with temper and she had never seen his jaw set in such an uncompromising line.

'If you wanted to show what you think of me,' he grated, 'couldn't you have been more personal about it instead of involving the company?'

'What are you talking about?'

'The dinner for Voegler.' He reached out and caught her shoulders. 'Did you have to ruin it? Was it because Jackie didn't want you to come. Is that why you did it?'

'Did what?' Lizbeth cried. 'You're not making sense to me.'

'You make plenty of sense to me,' he grated. 'I'm just beginning to see what you are. Rotten, evil and——' He flung her away from him, the gesture so violent that she fell against the wall.

A sharp pain shot through her shoulder, but she ignored it, intent on trying to understand what Danny was saying. 'What am I supposed to have done?'

'The worst thing you could have done—and you succeeded brilliantly.' Pale eyes stabbed at her. 'There was the most almighty row and Rexham walked out swearing he'd never write a word about Voegler and that as far as he was concerned, N.A.T. no longer existed. Then Durford had a set-to with a couple of other critics and——'

'Durford?' she gasped. 'But I never invited *him*. You didn't think I ... *You can't think that?*'

'Then who did?' Danny leaned towards her. 'You won't pretend you don't know they hate each other's guts, and you were the one who made out the interview list?'

'Of course I made it out,' she said angrily, 'and I know my job well enough never to invite Durford with J.D. I said as much to Mrs Allen when I gave her the list.'

'You said it to cover yourself,' Danny shouted. 'But you had every intention of making sure Durford was there.'

'I told you I didn't invite him!'

'He had a letter from you. He told me so.'

Lizbeth backed into the living-room and groped for the nearest chair. 'What letter? How could he have had a letter from me when I never sent him one?'

'For God's sake stop lying!' Danny exploded. 'You've had your victory—why not be honest with yourself and gloat!'

'I've nothing to gloat about,' she cried. 'Why should I want to hurt you by ruining Voegler's press party?'

'Because getting Voegler here was my responsibility, and turning his party into a shambles was the one thing guaranteed to upset him and make a fool of me.' Danny gripped her shoulder again and shook her backwards and forwards. His face was livid with fury and she had the impression that he was too enraged to know what he was doing. 'From the moment you met me you lost your sense of humour,' he rasped. 'You couldn't stomach the fact that I played a joke on you and you built me up as an ogre that you had to destroy!'

'I never built you up into anything. I never even gave you a thought!'

'Is that why you've always gone out of your way to rebuff me every time I've tried to be friends with you?'

'I don't want your friendship,' she stormed. 'I work for your company, but that doesn't mean I have to kow-tow to you like every other girl in your employ. That's why you're angry with me, isn't it? Because you know I despise you.'

'You have no reason to despise me.' He was still angry but he was no longer shouting. 'You're a sick girl, Lizbeth. Sick and warped.'

'How dare you say that?' she gasped.

'I'm doing it for your own good.' He glanced around at Don, who had silently listened to every word. 'She's your girl-friend. You control her. If it weren't for the fact that more publicity would be involved, I'd sue her for what she did tonight.'

'Lizbeth said she didn't do it.' Don was pale and looked nervous, but he came to stand close beside her, as though wanting to comfort her. 'You obviously have your reasons for believing she wants to get even with you, but from what I know of Lizbeth she isn't the sort to do anything mean or spiteful.'

'Then your opinion differs from mine.' Danny glared at Lizbeth again. 'Come to the office in the morning and clear out your desk. Forget your three months' notice. As far as I'm concerned I don't want you ever to set foot inside Amalgamated.'

'You can't dismiss Lizbeth like that,' said Don. 'Even a criminal is allowed a trial, and you're judging her without giving her a chance to defend herself.'

'I don't want to hear any more.' Danny looked infinitely weary. 'You should have been at the party tonight, then you'd understand how I feel.'

Before Don could reply he was pushed to one side and Danny strode out. But his anger remained with them, reverberating in the atmosphere.

'I never invited Durford,' Lizbeth whispered. 'Everyone knows he and J.D. are enemies.'

'*Someone* invited him,' Don pointed out. 'Could your secretary have done so by mistake?'

'No. I gave her the list myself.'

'Who else knew about it?'

'No one. I wrote out the names and gave them to Mrs Allen on a sheet of paper. She typed out the letters and I signed each one myself.'

'It might be interesting to see Durford's letter. That might give you a clue as to who signed it.'

'Who would want to make mischief for Danny?'

'Equally to the point,' said Don, 'who would want to make mischief for you?'

It took a moment for the meaning of the question to register with Lizbeth, but when it did, it gave her a different view of things. Don was right—the mischief tonight not only affected National Amalgamated but herself too. And this was not the first time she had been put in the wrong as far as Danny was concerned. There had been her failure to meet Kurt Voegler at the airport. That mishap had also been caused by a wrong message.

'Who hates you enough to want to hurt you?' Don asked. 'Anyone in your office?'

Lizbeth shook her head, unable to credit any of her staff with such behaviour. Yet if both the Voegler mishaps were deliberate acts of mischief then the same person could be responsible. She turned and went into the sitting-room. Kurt Voegler's arrival at London Airport had been common knowledge, but the party at the Savoy had been deliberately kept quiet, and only she and her secretary had known whom she had invited. She cast her mind back to the day when she had written out the list of names. She had done it at her desk, then handed the list to Mrs Allen, who—Lizbeth gasped and stared at Don.

'Jackie was in my office when I was talking to Mrs Allen about whom to invite. I told her about J.D. and Durford.' She moistened lips that were suddenly dry. 'But why would she do it? It doesn't make sense.'

'Yes, it does. She's frightened of you. The very fact that she didn't want you at the party tonight proves it.'

'Her reason for that wasn't wrong,' Lizbeth felt bound to say. 'And she certainly isn't frightened of me. I'm not an actress.'

'But you *are* her rival.' Don looked grim. 'I told you in Switzerland that I thought Danny fancied you. Jackie thought so too. She watched him like a hawk the whole time. Work it out for yourself.'

'It's crazy! He loves her.'

'She's still jealous of him—whatever she might say to the contrary.' Don glanced at his watch and then went over to the telephone. 'What's Durford's number?'

Automatically Lizbeth gave it to him and listened as he dialled. His conversation was short, but he put down the receiver with a satisfied expression. 'Come on,' he said, 'we're going out.'

'Where to?'

'To take a look at Durford's invitation.'

Twenty minutes later Lizbeth and Don faced the eminent critic and writer in his book-lined study. He was a tall, thin man with a sharp-featured face.

'So you're the girl who misinvited me to meet Kurt Voegler?' he said, favouring Lizbeth with a stony glance. 'I can't think why I agreed to meet you except that I'd like to thank you for giving me the chance of spoiling J.D.'s indigestion.'

'Lizbeth didn't invite you,' Don said before she could reply. 'That's why we're here. Lizbeth's as professional in her job as you are in yours. She wouldn't make such a stupid mistake—even though you enjoyed it!'

'Indeed?' Durford opened a drawer. 'Here's the letter that came from her. See for yourself.'

Don took the envelope and with precise movements, careful only to touch the edges of the letter, extricated it and lowered it to Lizbeth's eye level.

'That's not my signature,' she muttered, 'but it's an excellent copy.'

'Are you sure?'

'Positive.'

Don looked at Durford. 'Who else has held this letter?'

'No one except me.'

'Would you swear to that?'

The man looked thoughtful and then nodded and watched Don slip the envelope and letter into his pocket. 'What are you going to do with it?'

'Take it to a friend of mine at Scotland Yard and have it examined for fingerprints.'

'Now that will make a good story. I assume you would wish me to write about it if you can prove whatever it is you're trying to prove?'

'If it shows what I think it will,' Don said grimly, 'I'm afraid we won't be able to get any publicity out of it. It's something we'd want to hush up.'

The sharp eyes examined Lizbeth appraisingly. 'I suppose it's a personal vendetta? Well, I wish you luck.'

'We'll need luck,' Don muttered to Lizbeth as they returned to the car. 'When you went to meet Voegler at the airport, who gave you the time he was arriving?'

'I told you. Mrs Allen left a note on my desk for me.'

'You wouldn't still have it, would you?'

In the act of shaking her head, Lizbeth stopped. There was a slim chance that she still had it in her handbag.

'Let's go and check,' said Don, and set the car once more in the direction of her flat.

Arriving there she went immediately to her wardrobe and took out the suede shoulder bag she had worn that day she had gone to the airport. She used it rarely because it showed fingermarks and since that day, had not taken it out again. She opened the bag, tilted it up and shook it. It was empty and she was in the act of putting it back when she heard a rustle. Thinking she had left some paper money in the purse, she unzipped it. It was empty save for a folded sheet of white paper. It was the typewritten note from Mrs Allen.

'I've found it!' she called, and ran into the living-room.

Don took it from her carefully and slipped it into the envelope with the letter. 'Now we go and see my friend,' he said. 'I'll check first to make sure he'll be there.'

A short telephone call later, Lizbeth and Don left the flat for the third time that evening and headed towards New Scotland Yard.

'I feel as if I'm stock footage in a T.V. series!' she said wryly. 'The kind of film where they keep repeating the same section of a scene to fill in time.'

'Don't remind me,' Don grinned. 'I've acted in enough of them.' He slowed at the lights and looked serious again. 'I'm counting on finding Jackie Elton's fingerprints on the letter that was sent to Durford.'

'And the typewritten note too?' Lizbeth asked hopelessly.

'Why not? It's feasible. After all, she came out of your office and saw the note Mrs Allen had left on the typewriter for you. It wouldn't have taken her more than a minute to type another one giving you the wrong time to meet Mr Voegler.'

'I can't believe she would do such a thing. I can understand her disliking me because she's jealous of Danny, but to deliberately try and ruin me—for that's what it will do to my career—seems so evil.'

'Jealousy can make one evil—or at least bring it out if it's there.'

'We'll have to get Jackie's prints before we could prove it,' said Lizbeth.

'I already have them. I brought her back from Elstree a few weeks ago and she left her compact in the car. We'll be able to compare the prints on that with the ones we find on the note and the letter.'

'It's a slim chance,' Lizbeth said, and this comment was echoed by Don's friend, Superintendent Brimmer, when they sat before him in his office at the Yard.

'If several people have handled that letter of Durford's, all the prints on it may be blurred,' he explained.

'Durford said no one else touched it except himself. And Liz and I only held it by the edge.'

'If we were to find Miss Elton's prints on them, would you wish to prosecute her?'

'Oh no,' Lizbeth said quickly. 'I only want to clear my name.'

'We aren't here officially, Jack,' said Don. 'I thought you'd help us as a favour.'

The Superintendent pursed his lips and then sighed. 'Leave it with me and I'll see what I can do. I'll be in touch with you.'

Don appeared satisfied with this statement,

though Lizbeth would have wished for something a little more positive.

'For old Jack, that remark *was* positive,' Don assured her as they returned to the car. 'He'll call me as soon as he finds anything.'

'I'll be in my office first thing in the morning to clear out my desk,' said Lizbeth. 'But I'll come straight back to the flat and wait to hear from you.' She squeezed his arm. 'I never realised how resourceful you were.'

'You never realised a lot of things about me.' His glance was rueful and she wished she could offer him more than friendship. With a sigh she climbed into the car.

CHAPTER THIRTEEN

EARLY in the morning—long before most of the staff had arrived at N.A.T.—Lizbeth was clearing out her desk. There were the usual toiletries to pack, several signed photographs of celebrities thanking her for her efforts on their behalf and some personal reference books which she occasionally leafed through when she was looking for ideas on which to build publicity hand-outs. It was amazing how many newsy situations she had derived from the *Guinness Book of Records*.

She dumped everything into a canvas hold-all and was in the act of zipping it shut when her telephone rang. It was Don.

'I called you at the flat. I didn't know you'd be leaving so early.'

'I wanted to get away from here before people arrived,' she explained.

'You don't need to sneak in and out like a thief.' His voice quickened. 'We've got the proof we wanted, Liz. Durford's letter was covered with Jackie's prints, and so was that typed note. In fact there was only two sets of prints on that one: yours and hers.'

'How do you know they were mine?' she asked, startled.

'I pinched your lipstick case from your handbag and left it with Jack!'

'And now?' she asked shakily.

'And now we go and see the delightful Miss Elton.'

This was the moment for which Lizbeth had been waiting, yet somehow she could not face it. What was the point confronting Jackie with what she had learned? Even if Danny apologised for wrongly accusing her, she could not go on working here. Hard on this thought came the realisation of what the truth would mean for him. How would he feel when he discovered that the girl he loved had resorted to such monstrous behaviour in order to destroy someone else's character? Obviously he would wonder why Jackie had done so and, because he was astute, would soon realise it had stemmed from jealousy. Once he had reached this conclusion, it would not take him long to guess that she was deeply attracted to him and that Jackie had been afraid she would become another of his girl-friends. Another of his girl-friends. The ignominy of knowing how nearly she had succumbed to him filled her with shame.

'You still there, Liz?' Don asked. 'I thought I'd come over with Jack's report and we could take it to Danny Ferguson.'

'I don't want to do anything about it.'

'What?' Don shouted the word. 'Are you out of your mind? After what he said to you last night, you should——'

'No, Don; I want to forget it.' Her voice was husky and she cleared her throat. 'I couldn't go on working here anyway, and there's no point raking over dead ashes.'

'Your good name isn't dead ashes,' he said angrily. 'You can't let Jackie get away with what she did.'

'I doubt if she'll repeat the operation. Once she's

married to Danny she won't feel the need to defend her position.'

'What about *your* position? Or isn't it important to clear yourself?'

'I'm going back to work for my father, Don. It won't matter what people here think of me.'

'News spreads,' Don said. 'If you leave like this, everyone will know it's because you were fired. Anyway, Ferguson should be told the truth.'

'He's already judged me,' she said bitterly. 'What's the point showing him he should have had more faith?' Her voice cracked and she tried to end the conversation before she burst into tears. 'Forget it, Don. I have the satisfaction of knowing it was Jackie and I'm happy to leave it like that.'

'I'm coming over to talk to you.'

'I'm going home, Don. Goodbye.' She put down the telephone, swiftly gathered her things together and left the building.

She half expected to find Don waiting for her at the flat, but there was no sign of him, nor did he try to contact her on the telephone. The morning passed slowly, each hour bringing with it the memory of what she would have been doing under normal circumstances: finding out how many pages they were being allocated in the next edition of the weekly T.V. Guide; going through the latest T.V. ratings to find their own top show and then trying to concoct stories either around the show itself or its participants; making her usual round of telephone calls to the national dailies and Sunday newspapers and then lunching with either an editor of a magazine or a feature writer in the hope that it would lead to an article. Obtaining publicity in magazines was an art in itself, and though it did not have the same immediate impact as a newspaper headline, it had a much more solid outcome. Readers of magazines were loyal and it was rewarding if they could be encouraged to give that loyalty to a singer or an actor or a show. Today her lunch guest would have been the editor of one of the glossies, whom Lizbeth had been prepared to offer an exclusive series of photographs of Jackie which had been taken in Switzerland and which showed the star's beautiful wardrobe, designed specially for her by a new Turkish dress designer. But from now on this would be somebody else's job. She was never going to think of television again.

The urge to go and see her parents was strong, but she resisted it. Besides, her mother was already in surgery and her father could be anywhere in London seeing people. It was better to wait until this evening before going to tell them all that had transpired in the past twenty-four hours. Without question they would not doubt her innocence, knowing her too conscientious to have made such a stupid mistake as to invite Durford and J. D. Rexham to the same party. But would they think she had behaved wisely in not confronting Jackie with the truth? It was too late to change her mind and she knew she would not have done so even if she had the opportunity.

Unexpected pangs of hunger made her realise she had rushed out this morning without having breakfast, and she started to prepare herself some lunch.

She was carrying a tray to the sitting-room—having decided it would be more comfortable to sit beside the electric fire than in the kitchen—when the doorbell rang. She looked at the cheeseburger and wondered if there would be enough for two. She ought to have guessed Don would come to the flat in search of her. Resting the tray against her hip, she crossed the hall.

'I won't change my mind, but I *will* give you lunch,' she said, opening the door.

'I'll accept that offer,' said Danny, and stepped into the hall before she could stop him.

'Get out!' she choked.

'I knew you'd give me a warm welcome.' He caught her by the arm and turned her so sharply that she almost dropped the tray.

'I want to talk to you,' he said, propelling her into the sitting-room. 'And I mean talk, not enter into a bar-room brawl!'

With a toss of her head Lizbeth set the tray on the table before turning to look at him. Never had he seemed so tall and dark nor so angry. His eyes sparkled and his jaw was clenching and unclenching, making a muscle come into prominence at the side of one cheek. She felt her own tenseness increase and her racing pulse made her breathless, forcing her to breathe in deeply. He noticed it and some of the anger left his face.

'Why didn't you come and tell me what you and Don had found out? Weren't you interested in showing me what a fool I'd been?'

'No. You thought me capable of—of...' She averted her head. 'Showing you that you were wrong didn't seem important.'

'Why?'

'Because I don't care what you think of me.'

'I'm sorry for what I thought,' he said violently.

'If it gives you any satisfaction I would like you to know that last night was one of the most miserable times in my life.'

His words should have appeased her bitterness, but somehow they didn't. The events of the last day had been so cataclysmic that she supposed she was still numb from them. All she could feel was an overwhelming need to be left alone.

'I appreciate your coming here to apologise,' she said. 'I realise it must have been difficult for you.'

'That was the easy part. The hard part is yet to come.' He came a step closer. 'I suppose you see me as the man who's always jumping to the wrong conclusions about you?'

'I once jumped to the wrong conclusion about you!' she made herself sound amused and was startled by the murmur of anguish which her remark elicited.

'I wish to heaven I'd never put on that act with you,' he said grimly. 'It started us off on the wrong foot and from that time on we've never been able to get on the right one. I still find it hard to understand why. It was unlike you not to see the funny side of it. When you sent me that snake I was staggered.'

'I didn't send it to you because you pretended to be an actor,' she blurted out—and then stopped, furious that her overwrought state had made her loosen her guard and say too much.

'Then why *did* you send it?' His hand came out and caught hold of her chin, forcing it round until she was facing him. 'Answer me, Lizbeth. What did I do that made you so furious with me?'

'I don't like flirts,' she said as calmly as she could.

'I never wanted to flirt with you,' he replied equally calmly. 'From the moment I met you I wanted to love you.'

'How can you talk like that when you're engaged to Jackie?'

'I'm not engaged to Jackie.' He dropped his hands, but only to lower them and place them upon her shoulders. 'I am not engaged to Jackie,' he repeated, 'and I never have been.'

'You're lying!'

'I am not.' He gave her a shake. 'So that's why you've been treating me as if I were a leper?'

'I don't trespass on other people's property.'

'I belong to no one except myself.' He shook her again, much harder this time, so that her teeth rattled. 'That still doesn't excuse you for not having lunch with me the first time I asked you out. You hadn't met Jackie Elton then.'

'I saw you together at a film premiere.'

'So what? I've escorted stacks of girls to film premieres, but that doesn't mean I'm engaged to them.'

'I heard you were,' she said. 'It was common gossip.'

'Gossip is generally common,' he snapped. 'Jackie and I were——'

'I don't care about your relationship with her! You're free to go out with a thousand different girls if you like.'

'I appreciate your open-mindedness,' he said ironically. 'But now that you know Jackie is not—and never was—my fiancée, does it make any difference to you?'

Pride gave her the ability to be flippant. 'It means I could go out with you with a clear conscience.'

'I take it that means you're willing to join the legion!'

She coloured. 'I said "could", Mr Ferguson, not "would".'

'I see.' His head lowered towards her. 'I've always enjoyed a woman's company and I saw no reason why I should deny myself that pleasure until such time as I only wanted the pleasure of *one* particular woman. You, Lizbeth Dawson.'

Her hair swung forward as she bent her head in an effort not to let him see her face. 'And how long can I look forward to being your particular fancy?'

'A lifetime,' he said huskily. 'I love you.'

Her head swung up sharply. 'Why me?'

'I must be a sadist! You've certainly gone out of your way to hurt me since we've met.'

'You never acted as if you were hurt,' she said bluntly. 'If Jackie wasn't around you took out anyone who was.'

'Because I wasn't going to let you know that you'd turned my life upside down. But none of them meant anything to me. Worse than that—they bored me to death! I couldn't wait to take them home and leave them. Leave them,' he reiterated, then paused before he said: 'Since meeting you I haven't wanted to do anything else.'

The thought of Switzerland with Jackie was too near for her to forget it, but before she could say so, he spoke again. 'Do I need to tell you what a liar Jackie is? I know I never took *your* word when you protested your innocence, but will you be more forgiving towards me and believe me when I say that from the time you came into my life, Jackie went out of it?'

'She had your cuff-links in her bedroom,' said Lizbeth.

His eyes did not flicker but regarded her steadily. 'I had an affair with her—I've never denied it. But it finished when I met you.' One dark eyebrow lifted and he looked mocking again. 'I must say I surprised myself. I hadn't realised I was so old-fashioned in my emotions. I only want you, Lizbeth. No one else, just you.'

He had moved slightly away as he had spoken and he still made no attempt to touch her. It was as if he was saying that he had declared his love and could go no further. If she wanted it, she must be the one to make the next move. With a murmur she took a step forward and rested against his chest. Only then, close to him, was she fully aware of the effort it had cost him to say what he had. He might look calm and amused, but his heart was racing faster than her own.

'I love you, Danny,' she whispered. 'That's why I was so hurt when you didn't believe in me.'

'If I loved you less I would probably have been able to trust you more,' he said as his arms slowly came up and around her.

'Life is going to be very difficult if you don't trust the girl you love,' she said whimsically.

'It only happened because I was so mixed up about you. I loved you, yet I was furious with you for not wanting me. I couldn't think straight and when it came to that meeting with Mr Voegler and Durford's letter, I couldn't think at all!'

She shivered. 'Don't let's talk about it any more.'

'No more jealousy of Jackie?'

'Only pity. I'll even be able to do her publicity.'

'You'll never do that! You aren't going back to work for N.A.T. It wouldn't be seemly for the Managing Director's wife to work for her husband's company.' His eyes narrowed as he saw the colour flame into her face and he gathered her into his arms, lifting her from the ground. 'Don't you know that's what I want? To marry you and to have you with me for the rest of my life?'

'I thought you wanted——' Emotion made it impossible for her to go on and she buried her head into the side of his neck. Here too a pulse was hammering and she pressed her lips to it feeling a tremor run through him at her touch. 'I thought you wanted me as your girl-friend.'

'I do, my darling, but also as my wife.'

Her arms lifted to cup his head, twining her fingers through his thick, springy hair. She pulled his face down until she could rest her lips against his, giving a soft cry of pleasure as she felt the warm pressure of his mouth. Expecting his passion, she was surprised by his tenderness and the gentle way he caressed her, nuzzling his cheek against hers, running soft kisses on her eyelids, the tip of her nose, the side of her cheek, his lips finally against her ear, nibbling the lobe.

'Are you one of those girls who wants a great big wedding?' he asked.

'I'd be just as happy to elope.'

'We can't do that,' he whispered regretfully. 'We'll have to have a few trimmings, and you must meet my parents and my sisters.'

'The thought scares me.' She pulled back from within the shelter of his arms and stared into his eyes. They did not hold the icy glitter she had often seen in them but were soft grey, and made more dark by the shadow of his lashes.

'I can't believe I'm going to marry you, Danny. It seems a dream.'

'You won't think that a month from now.'

'So soon?'

'I'd make it sooner if I could,' he said roughly, 'but I'm sure my father will insist on organising it all.'

'Do you think he'll like me? I'm not at all important.'

'You're the girl I love, and as far as my family is concerned, that makes you one of the most important girls in the world.'

She giggled. 'My mother always warned me not to marry an only son!'

'You've never taken other people's advice, have you, Lizbeth?' he teased, and pulled her close again, but almost immediately released her. 'I daren't go on holding you,' he said thickly. 'We're alone in the flat and I won't be responsible for my actions if you don't keep your distance.'

'If you want me——' she said shakily, and took a step towards him, stopping as he drew sharply back, his face strained.

'No, darling. When the ring is on your finger I'll make you mine.'

She smiled mistily. 'I never thought I'd hear you say something so old-fashioned!'

'Don't you like it?'

'I love it.'

'And I love you, Lizbeth my love, and will spend the rest of my life showing you how much.'

Choose from this list of Harlequin Presents editions

165	The Arrogance of Love	Anne Mather
166	Familiar Stranger	Lilian Peake
168	Dangerous Friendship	Anne Hampson
169	Cupboard Love	Roberta Leigh
170	The High Valley	Anne Mather
172	Roman Affair	Rachel Lindsay
173	Valley Deep, Mountain High	Anne Mather
174	The Burning Sands	Violet Winspear
175	Man without a Heart	Roberta Leigh
176	Tinsel Star	Rachel Lindsay
177	Smouldering Flame	Anne Mather
178	The Sun Tower	Violet Winspear
179	Sanctuary in the Desert	Elizabeth Ashton
181	Isle at the Rainbow's End	Anne Hampson
182	Unwilling Bridegroom	Roberta Leigh
183	Valley of the Vapours	Janet Dailey
184	A Man to Tame	Rachel Lindsay
185	Wild Enchantress	Anne Mather
186	A Bitter Loving	Lilian Peake
187	Hills of Kalamata	Anne Hampson
188	The Marquis Takes a Wife	Rachel Lindsay
189	Beware the Beast	Anne Mather
190	This Man Her Enemy	Lilian Peake
191	Strange Adventure	Sara Craven